TE
SCORE

DANIEL P. COUGHLIN

A HellBound Books LLC Publication

www.hellboundbooks.com

To Dan Ditmar: Thanks for getting me here.

This book would not have been written properly without the criticism of my dear friends Danny Homan, Cara Homan, Joffrey Mason, Bobby Hoyt, and my brother, also a brilliant writer, and partner in crime Ryan Coughlin. And to my son Kasey Max Coughlin – always buddy!

And thanks to my amazing yet terrified and leery parents John and Kristine Coughlin and my wife Kelli-Rae for their loving support.

Prologue

1

The Jefferson House reception hall was a badly painted white warehouse that sat off of Interstate 94 just outside the small town of Watertown, Wisconsin. The parking lot was a squared off patch of land covered with gravel purchased from the local quarry. Weeds shot up through the gray dirt beneath the dusty crushed rock because the city officials never approved financing for new blacktop. The fragrant pine trees surrounding the Hall were very green during the summer and the Maple trees had red and rustic-colored leaves in the fall. Just before sundown, if you looked from a distance, the Jefferson House appeared to be God's inspiration to Norman Rockwell.

During the icy Wisconsin winters, the Hall catered to the local snowmobile crowds that piled into the bar and lounge area, which was simply seven rows of picnic tables with bench seats. Most of the time, the bundled-up crowds still wore their blaze orange snowsuits while they drank heavy mugs of beer and shouted to one another in familiar tongue. Afterward, they would corral on their sleds and convoy down the iced-over Rock River, making their way to the next watering hole. And no one seemed to turn a cheek to the fact that these inebriated people shouldn't be operating anything that required a key to operate. In general, the Jefferson House served as a meeting place for locals, and it was an affordable place for the working-class people of Watertown to throw wedding receptions and anniversary parties—added to which—it could accommodate a healthy amount of patrons, up to two hundred. Small bar brawling and drunk driving tickets were the worst crimes to occur on any given Friday or Saturday night. Sometimes, the local law enforcement officials parked their squad cars at the mouth of the gravel drive near the freeway on-ramp. They'd wait for a swerve, or a beer bottle being tossed from a moving vehicle, then they'd *have you*.

Forest and tall grass hid the hall from common view and about a half mile down a small dirt path lay the Community Campgrounds—tucked in tightly near the man-made fishing pond.

Yet, there was one incident that haunted the Jefferson House and had done so for over two decades. Behind the cheers and smiles and beer-stained conversations that filled the friendly Hall was a dark tale, a rumor of foul play about a young couple that disappeared in the early 1980s. The young love birds, Joan Neverman and Rodney Schmidt, both aged eighteen, were never found after their visit to the Jefferson House. Amongst the warm-red-faced crowds of humble townies, silent conversation revealed the haunting incident.

The disappearance caused the town council to close down a few receptions while the investigation went on, but the place never lost any of its popularity or booking, and the Hall was always scheduled tight for at least six months in advance. Too many good times had been experienced at the Jefferson House to reflect on the bad and horrible thing that happened in years past. The thought that a great evil could reside, subtle and hidden, in the small town was very unlikely, to most.

2

Watertown, a stand-out small town of nineteen thousand, was merely two miles south of the Jefferson House and filled with Midwesterners proud of their community. A good percentage of the townsfolk were bottle workers at the local Cola Factory, which employed nearly four thousand workers. The job was simple, but it required patience, discipline, and good management. Respect for hard work was common opinion amongst the workers and families of the surrounding township. And at community sanctioned events it wasn't uncommon to see many employees wearing factory tee shirts and hoodies in support of the town's livelihood. Most of the townsfolk were of German or Irish descent, explaining the heavy drinking, which was very prevalent amongst even the most respected community members.

Neatly lined, nicely painted houses crowded in rows throughout the town limits and decorated the community with a safe feeling. Watertown was suburbia polished over with Midwestern elbow grease. The yards were mowed and watered regularly in the fall, spring, and summer.

Large, restored Victorian brick homes became evident two blocks from the downtown area where the nightlife always seemed to have a lively kick. There were enough bars running in the small town to hold every last member of the community and then some. Beer flowed and whiskey sank in the many dark taverns and pubs, which were illuminated with fluorescent blue, pink, green, and red colors that blared out for anyone *of age* to drop by for some hops. A few raggedy houses lined the back streets on the north side of town where the deviants seemed to cling together. The unemployed could easily find affordable housing, some of which was aided by the government. And stereotypically, most of the drugs that injected the town were distributed on those streets. Drugs weren't a major problem, but if one wanted an eight-ball of cocaine or a few pills of oxycodone—they could score fairly easy in the north part of town.

Grocery stores and shopping outlets presented themselves at the northeast end of Watertown and finally sealed the town limits from a twelve mile stretch of highway. The nearest town was Johnson Creek.

Chapter 1
The Incident in 1980

1

The popular rock band Queen blared out from the reception hall and every time the front doors opened, Ted Olson would hear hoots and drunken hollers escape the building along with a haze of cigarette smoke. The hoots and hollers were of those he wished to hunt. He'd hunted in Korea and killed many men. They were trying to kill him and therefore it was justified—killing them. It was different, what he was doing here now. These were *lesser beings* that he wanted to hunt now. The stalk and capture were the fun part and it excited Ted. His blood curdled and his weathered skin leaked sweat just thinking about what he could do with a young one. One with blonde hair, he liked those ones best. Doing *things* with their helpless and pathetic *beings* was a ritual he enjoyed. It didn't get him off like he imagined most people got off by what his mother called "intercourse"—but *forcing it* from them was something that words could not describe. It was powerful.

His heavy right forearm snuck up from the grass and slid across his creased forehead, wiping away the beads of sweat that threatened to trickle down his sun burned nose and tickle his thin upper lip. His dark brown eyes looked toward the entrance of the Jefferson House. He saw them, the young couple that he'd been talking to earlier in the night. They'd been ordering beers at the bar when Ted saw *her*. Her hair was silky-blonde, and her skin was slightly red, probably from too much sun, but it made her shine and brought out her piercing blue eyes and pearly white teeth. The boy she was with looked average, making her beauty stand out tenfold. That's what Ted assumed he was to her: a boyfriend. They snuck kisses throughout the night, and she seemed to trace his young face every few minutes with graceful glances from her perfect eyes.

"Having a good one?" Ted had leaned over to ask her after he'd set his drink down on the beer-soaked bar. He hated to smile. His teeth were crooked and stained from his twenty-year habit of chewing tobacco.

"Sure. Always nice to celebrate," the girl responded. "I'm Joan."

Her subtle voice gave him goosebumps. He liked throats and when she talked, he watched the skin of her neck stretch forward and up like she was delivering a sweet tune, like the ones his mother used to hum while she rocked him to sleep at night as a child. No one could replace his mother's sound. Mother's voice was a bit raspy, but it soothed him, and he missed it dearly. Until she died in the late fifties he had only been away from her once and that was when he served in the Marines during the Korean conflict. He was gone four years and wrote to her every day. She never liked the blonde girls, although she was blonde herself. She would say blondes were the devil with pretty hair.

Ted nodded to Joan and left the reception hall undetected. His plan needed to unfold.

Still silent, waiting in the grass, Ted licked his cracked lips when she walked under the lamp post, her tanned legs strutting forward underneath her light blue sundress. Wiping his wiry brown hair away from his forehead, he watched blonde hairs sticking up from the part in her straight. He assumed the humidity was causing it to frizz. She kept smiling at the boy and tried to hold his hand, but he seemed preoccupied and a little drunk. That was good. He liked the males to be a bit out of control. It was easier to spring at them—if need be—and they were less likely to attempt an escape. They would go along with what he wanted to do, until he cut them.

"Hold on, Joan. I got to piss," the boy called out as they neared the edge of the gravel parking lot where the grass began. A gathering of bushes was nestled a few feet past the parking lot near the tree line.

"Rodney! Why didn't you *go* before we left?" Joan hollered.

Rodney's laughter stabbed Ted's ears. His stream of urine flowed onto a small birch tree near the forest edge making a heavy pattering sound as it hit the leaves and branches. The mist of his urine came within centimeters of Ted.

Ted's belly rubbed against the tall grass as he pulled himself along the ground toward Joan, next to a blue Mustang with white racing stripes.

Probably the boy's.

Rodney's zipper whizzed up and he turned to Joan.

"You want to go to Stan's?" he asked. "I think he's having an after-bar."

"No, I'm kind of tired. We should go back to my place." "Are your parents home?" he asked.

"Nope, they're in Milwaukee . . . for the night," she said. Her lips stretched wide, again, exposing her perfect teeth.

Ted slithered to the edge of the parking lot. If the girl were to look down, she would have seen the .44 caliber Bulldog, a heavy revolver, in his right hand. His foot slid in the gravel and the boy must have heard him.

"Hey, what are you doing there?" he shouted.

The girl spun around and saw Ted lying belly down in the gravel. She jumped back as Ted lunged at her like a lion springing on a zebra. He pressed the barrel of his revolver against her temple and wrapped his bare arm around her chest, hugging her tight, the fat of her breast seeping through his fingers.

"What's the problem, mister? What did we do?" Rodney asked, brushing his shaggy brown hair away from his babyface. His hazel eyes looked gray under the lamplight.

Ted grabbed the girl's breasts and squeezed hard. The boy turned toward the entrance, probably seeking a helping hand.

"Get over here now, boy," Ted whispered. "You yell and I'll shoot her dead."

The boy hesitated, but then cautiously stumbled toward him with his hands drawn up near his shoulders, his fingers fanned out in surrender. His steps shortened when he got within three feet and Ted waved the gun into the woods behind them. Rodney's eyes fell to the girl; she nodded for him to proceed. He walked into the tree line while Ted and the girl followed closely.

"What do you want with us?" Joan asked. Her voice was clogged with tears and phlegm. Ted pushed her forward, certain that she could feel his erection plunging into the small of her back. Her breasts were medium sized—a handful—and set perfectly. His fingers swept across them, and he felt the top of her firm stomach.

She must take good care of herself.

The woods were dark, but he knew where to go and he moved swiftly while the boy stumbled on every branch that corrupted his path. The trees suddenly cleared, and Ted's white Chevy pick-up truck emerged into sight. The boy turned back to Ted for direction. Waving the gun forward, Ted kicked at him.

"Passenger side," Ted whispered.

Hesitantly, the boy moved around to the passenger side of the truck and got in while Ted pushed the girl in through the driver's side. Once they were inside, Ted stretched his right hand across the girl and forced the gun barrel into the side of Rodney's ghost-white face. Thin beads of sweat glistened on his forehead. His hazel eyes looked sad when he turned to Joan.

Ted's ears rang after he pulled the trigger.

The black blood and small fragments of shattered skull dripped down from the passenger side window.

The girl's screams were choked off when Ted's large hands wrapped around her throat. Her neck was slim, and it wasn't long before it went limp in his hands, then he turned the key in the ignition and started the truck. Ted didn't think anyone had heard the gunshot or the screams. He drove down the dirt path that led onto Briar Road, which skirted Watertown and ended near Ted's house five miles out of town on County Trunk A—a back county road that met Highway 26 which stretched across the entire back country of the state.

2

Ted drove up the weed infested driveway and swung around back where a large wooden barn stood next to a field of tall green grass. The barn was forty feet high, and the rotting wood held traces of fading red paint.

Ted's truck came to an abrupt halt when he pulled the emergency brake. Joan slammed forward and smashed her head on the dash. Her body slumped over onto the boy, and she stirred, slight moans and grunts escaping her. She opened her mouth and Ted saw dried saliva stuck to the corners of her full lips.

Ted hopped out of the truck, walked around to the passenger's side and yanked Rodney's corpse onto the ground.

It hit like a sack of bricks and his broken head leaked gore onto the driveway. Joan woke up when Rodney's body hit the dirt, aware now and panicking. Her coughs drew Ted's attention, and he reached inside the cab of the truck and grabbed her beautiful hair. With one tug, his massive strength shot her out of the truck, and she hit the ground six feet from the barn. She coughed loud and started to wail. Ted slammed his boot into the back of her head. Her knees gave out and her face planted into the ground. Ted dropped on top of her and continued to bash her face into the gravel.

"No! No! No!" she screamed and sobbed. "Don't hurt me anymore . . . I don't want to die."

Those were the magic words—the words that sprung the overwhelming sense of power through him . . . *no, no, no*. He loved those words. They felt good in his ears. They meant that he had control. His anger and hate riveted to max capacity and he pulled his overalls down, directing his erect penis into her soft, warm, vagina. Thrusting violently into her, vomit erupted from Joan's mouth while Ted climaxed. He rolled off of her and watched her heave into the dirt.

She turned to Rodney and continued to sob. Her shaky knees dragged along the dirt toward him. And she looked as though she'd forgotten about Ted.

"Don't be dead," she pleaded with Rodney's lifeless body.

Ted walked into the barn and brought an axe down from where it hung between two long nails driven into a stud attached to the wall. He watched Joan stand up and look around the yard. He assumed that the girl thought she had an opportunity to escape. And then she sprinted down the driveway toward the road.

Ted marched quickly toward her.

About halfway down the driveway, Joan's feet got tripped up on the gravel and she fell to her knees, scraping the skin off and leaving deep red streaks.

The axe rose above her head. Ted drove the metal blade into her back below her neck. A woofing sound escaped her mouth, and he pulled the axe free and raised it again, this time lofting it down into her right leg. It took two chops for the leg to separate from her body. The blood flow was magnificent. Heavy spurts spat from the femoral artery and painted the gray gravel black. The moonlight sparkled in the wet blood.

Joan extended her arms forward and pulled with all her might. Ted watched her crawl toward the end of the driveway, away from his playpen. That's what he called his land. It was *his playpen* where he did what *he* wanted. On this land, Ted was the executioner, judge, and the court. And the sentence was always the same. No one had ever beaten death in this place. Ted removed his overalls and stood naked in the moonlight. His bare feet moved shakily across the gravel, then he was behind her, slamming the axe into her, tearing her limbs apart. His excitement heightened with each spray of her blood. It covered his legs, torso, and his face when he split her neck open. Steam rose from her intestines and Ted smiled, even though the smell was potent.

Standing naked above her chopped body, he became aroused again and he masturbated. Pleasuring himself came with the kill. It was liberating to be standing above his creation—his art—and absorbing it. He climaxed quickly and lay down in the gravel and took in the night air.

3

Hours later, Ted dragged the bodies into his field, behind the barn, where he set them next to the six-foot-deep hole he'd dug earlier in the week. He shoved the dismembered bodies into the earth and watched them tangle at the bottom.

Ted held Joan's head in his hand and debated whether to throw it into the hole. He decided against it for now. There was more fun to be had with it.

In the barn, he set Joan's head on his metal workbench and grabbed a five-gallon drum of gasoline along with a book of wooden matches. Then he went back to the grave and poured it on his *score*.

The bodies went ablaze, and he watched with fascination as their skin burned and boiled in the fire. The smell rose into his nostrils, sweet and thick and pungent. The aroma reminded him of his first kill. She had been the hardest, but the best. He adored his mother dearly and that's why it was so hard. But she was the devil. She had been the one who'd taught him to spot the score. She was able to teach him of their evil ways because *she knew* their evil ways firsthand.

Melinda Olson was mostly a cold woman, but she was affectionate with Ted. She adored him and wanted the best for him. He had a destiny to fulfill. "You'll be better than that dirty old greaseball," she'd said of his father.

Walter Olson, Ted's father, was an electrician, a drunk, and a foul display of anything father-like. He and Melinda would fight day and night and there were beatings. Not from him beating her. Melinda would slap Walter. He would threaten to divorce her and leave. And then she would throw things at him. One time, she stabbed him in the shoulder with a cleaver. When they were through fighting, Melinda would drag Ted downstairs from his bedroom and make him look at his father. And if he looked unappreciative of what his mother was doing, he would be beaten too. Mother hit hard. She would hit Ted until her knuckles bled and thin flakes of dead skin ripped away from her fists.

At first, Ted felt sympathy for his father, but as the years pushed on, he felt ashamed of him. Walter hung himself in the barn on Ted's sixteenth birthday. It happened after another one of their fights. This time, Melinda had knocked him unconscious with a toaster oven. And while Walter was unconscious, Melinda had lowered his pants and sodomized him with a broomstick.

Ted was forced to watch.

"This is what happens to little girls, Ted. They get fucked. You're not a little girl, are you?" Melinda shouted. "There are three kinds of people in this world, Ted. There are the strong, the weak, and the ones that the strong don't mind."

When Walter awoke to what was happening, he shot his wide eyes toward Ted. Ted knew that his father was ashamed. That was the final straw. Walter didn't say a word. He stood shakily and removed the broom handle from his rectum before going into the barn and hanging himself from the rafters with an orange extension cord. It was then that Ted knew what had to be done with mother. He'd been taught that women were the devil and if Ted wanted to escape his father's fate, then he would have to carry out what needed to be done.

That day was the first time he had thought of it— killing mother remained a fantasy until after the war. Ted was twenty-two years old and honorably discharged. Young and happy, he was thrilled to be home with a bright future on the horizon. He'd even thought of becoming a police officer. And that's when mother turned on him. She'd slapped him hard, and he'd taken it. The look she'd given him afterward was what pushed Ted over the edge.

"You ain't gonna be a cop," she said while cackling at him.

Ted was scared. He was afraid of his mother and what she could do to him right now. Fresh home from the Frozen Chosen Reservoir where tough Korean soldiers had been trying to kill him for years, Ted was more afraid of what his mother would do. And she was looking at him the way she looked at his father, like he was pathetic.

As if she could read his thoughts, she backed him down with her stare.

"I thought you would turn out better than this," she said, gritting her tea-stained teeth. "You *are* your father. A little girl," she continued while walking toward the kitchen sink where her flower vase bathed in soapy water. She grabbed it and raised it out of the sink.

Ted's anger won the battle over his mind. Before he acknowledged what he was doing, the butcher's knife that he'd grabbed off the table next to the fresh baked bread was slicing deep into her neck, choking off her screams.

Ted spun her around, then reason sunk in. Panic seized him and he fumbled his hands over the deep slit in his mother's neck that was spurting dark crimson blood. He stopped fumbling when she put her hand to the side of his face. She wasn't fighting him, and her touch was gentle. They stared deeply into each other's eyes. Melinda nodded her approval before closing her eyes forever. She was the first to be buried in the field behind the barn.

4

Now, standing over the remaining flames that burned his newest scores, Ted filled the hole with dirt. Afterward, tired and aching, he went into the house and filled a five-gallon bucket with soapy water and washed the blood from his truck while the sun rose over his isolated property.

Before going to bed, Ted neatly placed Joan's head in the freezer with aluminum foil wrapped under the stump of her neck. He could have fun with her head for a day or so before it started rotting and smelled bad.

5

Two days later, Ted bought a newspaper from a small newsstand in front of the Watertown Library that told the tale of two missing teenagers, Rodney Schmidt and Joan Neverman. The police had no leads and there were no witnesses. The newspaper was dated August 17th, 1980—another bookmark for Ted.

Chapter 2
The Benton's

1

At the south end of Watertown on the edge of James Street, Mary Benton watched the sun rise over the snow frosted field just inside the city limits. Even now, in March of 2010, the view from the kitchen window was just as nice as when they had moved in in 1988. The morning coffee burped and bubbled behind her. The dark roast smelled good, and she went to fill her mug. She used the same mug every morning, the one with the caption reading "Forty Is Twice As Great As Twenty."

"Morning, mom," Jules Benton called out when she entered the kitchen, busily texting away on her cell phone.

Jules' room was down the hall, across from Mary and Richard's master bedroom. It was a small home, only three bedrooms, but Mary loved it and was proud to live with her beloved family in it.

Mary was annoyed by her daughter constantly jabbing her fingers into the keypad of her Blackberry cell phone, probably because she didn't understand how to use the damn thing. A nosy and caring mother, on numerous occasions she had tried to sift through the channels of information on her daughter's phone but had ultimately been unsuccessful. This frustrated her. When she was a girl, all her parents had to do was listen-in on the telephone or merely refuse her privacy. It wasn't like that anymore. Now-a-days, kids have more rights, and they were treated like adults at a younger age. Mary didn't like that her seventeen-year-old daughter was going on thirty. Also, being a nosy parent was a good way of getting to know what was happening in her child's life. Technology was getting in the way of that. It was too easy for kids—not adults—to have privacy in the modern world. Unless you were willing to spend time grueling over the marvels of modern technology, which she was not. In her opinion, technology was diluting human contact.

Jules laughed as she walked past her mother, heading toward the coffeemaker. "Do you mind if I have dinner at David's house tonight?"

"Are you talking to me?" Mary asked, not knowing if Jules had some kind of strange earpiece stuck in her head or if maybe she was still talking on her cell phone.

"Yes, who else would I be talking to?" Jules spouted back.

"You know how your father likes to have family dinner, sweetie."

"I know, but David said he would make glazed salmon." Jules finally made eye contact with her mother. "And we need to talk about what we're going to wear to the spring formal. It's only a couple months away. I want to wear a custard slip, but we can't figure out what he should wear . . . without looking gay . . . to match it."

Mary shook her head and stifled back remarks about how trivial and unimportant Jules sounded. Then she remembered, briefly, that she had once been a teenager too and her concerns were much different *then* than they are *now*. Life certainly had a sick sense of humor. Her beautiful daughter's only concerns were matching attire for her and her boyfriend, while even though in the best shape she could possibly be in, Mary suffered from constipation and hadn't had a good bowel movement in two days. Her stomach was rolling, and sharp pains stabbed at her insides. Richard had wanted to make love the night before last, and she'd had to decline. After explaining that she was constipated, Richard had shrugged his shoulders and rolled over to his side of the bed.

"I guess you could eat dinner with the Millers," Mary finally responded.

Jules lowered her head to the screen of her Blackberry and whispered, "They won't be there."

"Who won't be there?" Mary asked while resting her knuckles on the countertop and straightening her arms.

"David's parents are up north at their new cabin. They know I'm coming over. Please? His parents are cool with it," Jules pleaded.

"You know what your father thinks about that."

"I know," she whined. "I just want to have a nice dinner . . . alone. Is that really too much to ask?"

Mary shook her head while she scooted around the counter toward Jules and hugged her. "I guess we could let you have dinner. Just make sure you're home by ten o'clock. It's a school night and you need to do your homework."

"I promise. Yeah," Jules said, clapping her hands.

Spoiling Jules was not Mary's intention, but it felt great to see her daughter so happy and lively. If she told Richard about Jules' plans while he was leaving for work, then he might be too preoccupied to debate whether or not Jules should be allowed to have dinner with David unsupervised. And Mary loved living vicariously through her daughter. It reminded her of the excitement that came with dating and youth. And what would it hurt? Up until now, she hadn't been a trouble to anyone. Her grades were good, all A's and she was athletic—a starting forward for the Watertown High School soccer team. She hadn't gotten pregnant yet, and Mary was certain that she didn't do drugs. She liked David, he was polite and charming. She also understood why Richard wasn't particularly fond of him. There was a wild side to the boy. Sometimes he was too polite and persuasive. Mary had to wonder what other kinds of things he was able to talk Jules into, when they were alone. Maybe it wasn't the best idea to let Jules go. On the other hand, they couldn't keep her trapped forever, just until she was eighteen.

Jules sat down at the kitchen table and stirred sugar substitute and cream into her coffee. Again, she was tapping away at her Blackberry. She chuckled every few minutes and Mary found herself wanting to know what was so funny. She felt left out. Mary's stomach rumbled. She rubbed it. Maybe the prune juice had kicked in and she would be able to have a nice bowel movement today. She hoped. Jules didn't have to worry about being constipated. She was young and beautiful. Her hair was silky, blonde, and shiny and her skin glowed with a nice tan.

She got her skin from Richard.

Glancing down, Mary noticed how short and revealing Jules' jean-skirt was. For a moment, Mary didn't know if Jules was wearing underwear or not. Her thong was so tiny that she couldn't see it. Also, girls were shaving *everything* these days and it was hard to tell if everything was being covered up or not. Mary had shaved her pubic hair once, because she thought that Richard might like it. It had turned him off incredibly.

They had been lying in bed about to make love when Mary removed her panties to show Richard her surprise. Naked with her legs up in the air, Richard had been a little embarrassed. After they made love, he'd said that it looked like an adolescent child's vagina. From then on, she kept trim, but didn't shave.

2

Richard Benton stood in front of the small rectangular mirror in the master bathroom flossing his teeth. He had a nice set of teeth that accentuated his chiseled jaw and masculine good looks. He'd aged very well. The crow's feet that stretched out from the corners of his eyes were the only real signs of aging on his face. His dark complexion brought out the blue of his eyes. Richard's wife, Mary, had aged well too. In fact, he felt lucky to have such an attractive wife. In her forties, she was still a knock-out. Even when Mary was pregnant, she didn't gain too much weight. And after the pregnancy, she'd kicked up her workout routine. She was a runner with nice, toned legs. They still made love often, not every night like they did when they were young, but at least once a week, which he thought to be healthy. Her backside was also very shapely, and he was thankful for that. Mary was more than a physical beauty. She was intelligent, funny, and easy to talk to. The intimacy that he shared with her was much deeper than sex. They had no inhibitions with each other, and they talked freely, often able to finish each other's sentences. They bickered, but rarely fought. They had their share of arguments, but nothing that would deem their marriage unsuccessful. And after Jules was born, they'd seen eye to eye on most parental issues. If they disagreed over anything, a simple talk in private would suffice. They rarely debated in front of Jules. There had only been a few times, like when Jules wanted to go camping up north at the Wisconsin Dells two summers ago. There were going to be boys with them, and Mary thought it would be okay. Richard had overreacted in front of both

Mary and his daughter. There was no way he was going to let his daughter go camping with boys. He knew what kinds of things would be going on—he was a teenager once too—and he wasn't going to allow his daughter to be put in a situation like that.

What kind of a father would he be if he allowed that?

He finished rinsing his mouth and went into the bedroom to put his work uniform on: thick black pants and a button down blue shirt with brown steel-toed boots. He'd been working at the bottling factory on the West end of town for twenty years and he enjoyed his job. Starting as a bottler when he was twenty-one years old and moving his way up to supervisor and now manager, he knew the factory inside and out. Not a job existed in the factory that he didn't know how to operate and maintain. There were thirty employees under him, and he was professional with all of them. Always wearing the proper uniform and keeping it nice and clean. It showed that he had pride. He even had his uniform drycleaned on a weekly basis.

The smell of coffee drifted into his nostrils as he walked down the hallway past his daughter's bedroom. He stopped for a moment to peek inside but saw no one. The bed was nicely made with tight, neat, hospital corners. He'd taught Jules how to make her bed when she was very young. His parents had been sticklers for neatness, but he hadn't learned how to make hospital corners until Navy bootcamp.

"Good morning, honey," Richard said, entering the kitchen.

He walked over to Mary and kissed her on the mouth. "Where's Jules?"

"She's in the living room watching the news . . . or jabbering on the text messaging . . . one or the other."

Richard grabbed her butt cheeks and squeezed. "Not bad, old lady. Not bad." He kissed her mouth again, hard, with passion.

"What's gotten into you lately?"

"What, I can't find my wife of twenty-three years attractive?" he asked. He knew that she felt good about herself, but he liked to say nice things that made her feel sexy. If she felt sexy then she would act sexy and that would keep them both happy. "Maybe tonight we could continue on from last night?"

"I think that could be arranged. And we'll be alone tonight . . . oh, that reminds me—I forgot to tell you that I told Jules she could eat dinner at the Miller's house. David and Jules want to coordinate their spring dance attire. I meant to ask you, but I didn't want to bother you with fashion issues."

Richard looked at his watch. It was seven-thirty and he needed to get to the factory. "I guess that would be fine."

"And it will give us a chance to be alone for a while," Mary included.

"Sounds good," Richard said and kissed his wife goodbye.

"Have a nice day, hon," she returned.

Richard shouted into the living room, "Have a good day at school, Jules!"

"You too, dad!" Jules called back.

Richard was out the door.

It was a nice sunny day, and the temperature was in the mid-forties. Winter had been freezing and snowy. And now, he was glad that the snow had started to melt. He could see patches of grass popping up on the lawn again. In another month he'd be able to mow it. He jumped into his black Ford truck and turned the key. The engine rumbled to life. He pulled out of the driveway and began his ritualistic morning prayer. He liked to pray while driving. He could look out the front windshield of his truck and admire the blue sky and bright sun. It made him feel special to know that God had given him such a wonderful life with plenty to be grateful for. His wife amazed him daily and he adored his precious daughter— brat that she was. Things hadn't always been great, but they had never been extremely bad either. Richard wanted to keep things that way. The only element of Richard's life that was slightly bothering him, these days, was David Miller; Jules' boyfriend.

He didn't care for the guy, and he didn't understand why Jules had so much affection for him. David was far from the man that he wanted Jules to be with. The guy was polite and said the right things, he looked clean-cut and decent, but there was something underneath the fabric of his nature that bothered Richard.

Once, while sitting at the dinner table, David had ordered Jules to get him a glass of milk. It was a simple request that didn't seem to bother Mary in the slightest, but it struck a chord with Richard. It was the mandatory tone in his voice. And he didn't say please. He just barked an order and Jules had popped to it. What else would David be capable of ordering his daughter to do? The thought chilled Richard's bones and he had to shake out the image of his daughter being ravaged by that punk. He knew that he could be wrong—the thought crossed his mind, but it didn't convince him.

Richard pulled his truck around to the rear of the bottling factory near the executive offices where management and the administrative personnel parked. He hopped out of the truck and prepared to execute his daily responsibilities.

Chapter 3
Telling Penny

1

Penny Sloan's white VW Jetta pulled into the Benton's driveway at seven forty-five. Jules' Blackberry chirped with the text message *HERE*. Smiling, she popped up from the brown reclining chair in the living room and skipped through the kitchen toward the garage door. Mary stepped in her way and forced a hug and kiss.

"I'm gonna be late," Jules said.

Just a little frustrated, Mary perked up and crossed her arms. "I got you off the hook for dinner tonight with your father."

"I'm sorry," Jules answered. "I didn't mean it." She wrapped her arms lovingly around her mother and squeezed. "Thank you . . . thank you . . . thank you."

The feel of her daughter's warm body reminded her of when Jules was only a part of her body. In the womb was where Mary first fell in love with her daughter.

"Love you mom," Jules said.

"I love you too," Mary answered and then Jules was out the door. Mary walked to the living room window and watched the two best friends exchange a short kiss on the cheek and shout out with excitement.

2

The white Jetta was littered with empty energy drink cans and coffee cups. Jules kicked them aside while they backed out of the driveway and drove to school. It was a short three miles, but it was nice to have a few minutes to chat with her best friend of twelve years. They had gone from kindergarten to high school together and there wasn't much that they didn't know about each other. Penny was dating Mark Tisdale, who was quarterback for the Watertown Thunder Bolts. He wasn't very good at football, but his leadership was enough for him to get the starting position. At least that's what Jules assumed. She'd grown up watching the Green Bay Packers every Sunday. She didn't necessarily enjoy the games as much as her father did, but she liked spending Sunday afternoons with dad. She was his baby girl and she loved to learn about the game in order to impress him. She'd picked up most of her football education listening to her father yell at the television. Brett Favre had left the Packers a few seasons ago, but she really liked the new guy, Aaron Rodgers. He was an underdog that had been able to overcome a good amount of adversity. Penny's boyfriend was only in high school—Jules understood that—but he was too cocky, and he didn't make smart throws on the field. Jules suddenly realized that she knew way too much about football, for a girl.

Penny pulled a Marlboro cigarette from a half-empty pack and pushed in the car's cigarette lighter. "So, what are we doing tonight?"

Jules smiled big and her cheeks flushed red. "David is making me dinner."

Penny frowned while she extracted the cigarette lighter from the ashtray and lit up. Smoke wafted up and out the driver's side window in thin streaks. "What's so great about that? Mark cooks for me all the time."

"His parents are out of town until Sunday."

"Oh, so there's gonna be a little unsupervised kiss-kiss grab-grab?" Penny asked, then blew smoke into Jules' face.

Jules took the cigarette from Penny and drew a long drag. Coughing hard as she exhaled, she said, "We're gonna . . ." Cough, cough. "We're gonna have sex."

Penny began hacking. "You're gonna fuck? Are you gonna pop your cherry or just give him the backdoor?"

Ashamed, Jules shook her head, then forced another drag off the cigarette. "No, I don't do . . . that."

"Why not? Everybody does. It's like having sex without having sex. It feels kind of good actually. I let Mark have the backdoor all the time. I think he likes it better than my vag."

Jules lowered her head. "I think I love David."

"What does love have to do with the backdoor?"

Jules slapped Penny's arm hard. "You're an idiot, my dear."

They arrived in the school parking lot. Penny drove around toward the football field where she liked to park because it was closer to her first hour chemistry class.

The car sputtered to a stop. "I love you Jules . . . and I know you're excited, it's very obvious. But . . . are you sure you're ready for this?"

Jules swore that she sensed genuine feelings from her delivery of the question, a rarity with Penny.

"Weren't you ready when you had your first time?"

Penny slowly shook her head. Her eyelashes began to moisten. "No. I wasn't ready, but I did it anyway. It wasn't special. It was with Ben Klug in the back of his Chevy . . . at one of Todd Rosner's farm parties."

"Well, why'd you do it then?" Jules asked inquisitively.

"Because I was curious as hell and he was hot, that's why! His breath was awful, and he lasted about two seconds."

"I hope David isn't like that. We've been talking about it for a while now . . . and we think that we're both ready. He bought condoms and everything."

"Awwwww . . . good for him. What a sweetie." The sarcasm was unmistakable. Then she quickly sat up straight. "Are you on the pill?"

"No, that's why we're gonna use the condoms."

"Just be careful. I had an abortion once. I take the pill religiously now."

Jules put her hand to her mouth and cringed.

"Don't look at me like that . . . that's terrible," Penny said as she reached into her cigarette pack and drew another smoke.

"I'm sorry, I didn't mean it. I just . . . I couldn't have an abortion. I would have to have it."

Penny shook her head and laughed. "Well, when it happens to you . . . then it's a different story, little lady."

And with that, they both exited the car and walked through the back entrance.

3

The hallways were bright with fluorescent lighting. The red lockers stood out against the white walls. Penny dropped off near the glass doors and went to her chemistry class while Jules continued walking toward her locker, near the cafeteria. She said hello to a few friends but didn't stop to talk much. She was becoming more nervous and excited by the minute. Losing her virginity was becoming more and more real, by the minute. The way some of her friends talked about it, sex wasn't such a big deal. But to Jules, it seemed like this was something that would be life altering. The thought of being intimate with David was turning her on, but at the same time it made her stomach turn and her forehead perspire. She hoped that it would be as special as she'd played it in her head. She also hoped that she didn't smell *down there*. And the thought of God watching her sent an uncomfortable shiver down her spine. But if they made love for all the right reasons, then it would be an act of love, not just meaningless teenage sex.

Her father was always preaching to her about not having sex until after marriage. It was a sin according to the bible. Jules took a deep breath and shook off the thought of religion altogether. She'd only be young once.

Best not to spend it stressed out. That's what grown-ups did.

Jules got to her locker and spun the combination right, left, right, then slid the handle up to reveal her neatly organized schoolbooks aligned in two separate categories. One row, the top one, was for her textbooks and the other was a small row on the bottom for her notebooks. She grabbed her Advanced Algebra book and the appropriate notebook and shut her locker.

She jumped, startled, when David appeared behind her. For the first time since they'd been together, she felt incredibly intimidated by his presence, and it seemed as though a ticking-time-bomb was staring at her. Here he was, this beautiful boy, and he was going to be making love to her in a few hours. They would be naked and vulnerable and most of all inexperienced. Well, she was inexperienced. He'd been with a few girls before her.

Fumbling his words he said, "Hey, Jules . . . you look, different . . . I mean really good. How do you feel?" His smile was big, and his face looked sweet. He had baby cheeks and heavy eyebrows set just below his crew-cut dark auburn hair. His body was very skinny, but she didn't care. The thing that turned her on was how special he made her feel. He cared for her and wanted to know everything about her—or so she assumed. He asked a lot of questions about her and always wanted to know how she felt.

"I'm good. How are you?" Jules asked back.

Her lips were trembling, and she knew that her cheeks were starting to flush. She hoped that David didn't think she was stupid. "I'm a little nervous. You're not?" David asked. Then he looked around the hallway as if he didn't want anyone to hear him.

"Yeah I am!" she belted out before covering her mouth, becoming aware that she had just shouted. Her face turned bright red, and David laughed at her. He grabbed hold of her shoulders and hugged her.

"I can't believe I just did that."

"It's okay. I feel the same way. There's about a million things I want to yell right now. You don't want to back out or anything, do you?"

She shook her head *no* slowly and slid her head close to his ear and whispered, "I can't wait for tonight."

Her face went red again. She couldn't believe that she'd just said that, and now David's face went from pinkish tan to bright red. She shut her locker and walked away, turning back—once—to smile sheepishly at her love. As she walked down the hallway toward algebra class, she was tingling all over, and she liked it. She yearned to be with David.

Chapter 4
The First Time

1

David Miller sat on his black leather chair watching pornographic images on his Mac computer. His parents never checked his website browser history. In fact, they were easy-going when it came to his privacy, and he appreciated that. Some of his other friends had parents who checked their web history and invaded their rooms constantly. The images on the computer were of a tanned blonde girl with two athletic looking boys, also very tan and young. The young girl was kneeling in front of a white sofa and there were many windows in the background. David could feel himself rising beneath his new Levi blue jeans while images of doing these things to Jules swam in his mind. He didn't want another person to be there having sex with Jules, but he wanted to engage in these acts with her—having her from behind, putting it in her mouth. He didn't think that she would be as excited as the girls on his computer seemed, but it would be more than he'd ever done.

The feelings David carried for Jules were strong. Degrading her wasn't something that he wanted to do to her. It was the acts and positions that he wanted to experiment with, but he was fairly certain that she wouldn't go for that. Jules' father was a Born Again Christian and David knew that he didn't care for him very much. David couldn't think of a reason that Mr. Benton shouldn't like him. There was one instance when David had told Mr. Benton that he doubted God's existence and that some Christians were so wrapped up in living according to the bible that they missed out on life. And that hadn't gone over well. In hindsight, it probably wasn't something he should have said to his new girlfriend's father either. But it was true, and he wanted Mr. Benton to know where he stood on the topic before they started going on food drives for the local Baptist Church. David gathered that Mr. Benton believed that all those who didn't believe in God and Jesus were doomed to spend eternity in hell. David knew too many *good* people who didn't share this opinion, and it was inconceivable to think that they'd land a front row ticket in the big incinerator because they didn't believe in a higher power. Jules' father made David not *want* to believe in God. His own parents couldn't care less about going to church or serving an imaginary man and had never pushed the ideal on him. Personally, David didn't know what he believed in. As of late, it seemed that the popular opinion was that God, in fact, did not exist. Jules believed in God, Jesus, and probably the Easter Bunny.

She'd implied on numerous occasions that if David came around to *believing,* that their relationship would become much stronger, spiritually and emotionally.

Right now, David wanted to focus on what he was going to do with Jules tonight. They'd been talking about having sex for months now. They had almost gone through with it one night at Mike Stelter's keg party, but David had had too many beers and they both decided that it would be a good idea to be sober when it happened for the first time. And then she had expressed her guilt for wanting to make love with him at all. It was everything that she was taught not to do. Her family and her pastor made sure that she knew how great of a sin it was to have intercourse before marriage. She'd even gotten mad at David for not taking her seriously while they talked about such issues. Jules wanted this experience to be special; *spiritual.* She wanted their bodies and minds to become one and David finally agreed. Not that he bought any of the bull she was dishing, but he respected her. He told her that it would be everything she wanted and expected. Then she talked about spending their lives together forever and how this would be some kind of bond. David thought he agreed.

It was about a week ago that David's mother had knocked on his door, opened it, and told him that the cabin they'd just bought needed some repairs and that she and David's father would be gone the following week.

"Your father and I bought a foreclosure up north on Lake Michigan. We need to go up there for a week and close the deal and maybe straighten the place up a bit.

Do you think you can handle being home by yourself for a week?" she asked with a light-hearted grin.

"I think I can handle that," David told his mother, smiling wryly.

"I was pretty sure you wouldn't mind." She smiled back and closed the door.

The first thoughts that came to David's mind were that he and Jules would now have a private place to get busy—to carry out their fantasies without worry of being caught.

David told Jules of his parents' future absence and they immediately began debating the pros and cons.

Jules clammed up.

"I don't want to just have sex, David. I want it to mean something," she expressed.

He could tell that she didn't like the sly smile plastered to his face when he said that they could have a week-long sex-fest in his parent's house.

"I feel the same way," David told her, then held her while they sat on the bottom steps of the school library just before the last period of class that Friday.

David was surprised when Jules agreed.

"Okay. Do you think we're ready?" she asked him with a cute smile that reflected her innocence.

"I do. We've been talking about it for months and we are . . . we're ready."

Jules nodded and the day came fast.

2

When he heard the doorbell ring, David closed out the porn site, gave himself a quick look in the mirror, then walked to the front door. After sniffing his armpits, he opened the door for Jules. She looked gorgeous, as usual, and he asked himself silently how he could have scored such a beautiful girl. He knew that he wasn't the best man for her, but somehow, she wanted him. Her smile almost made him blush and her perfume was light, but very prominent. He kissed her gently on the mouth and stared into her hazel eyes.

"You hungry?" David asked.

Jules lowered her chin and raised her eyebrows. "I don't know." She smiled smugly. "I have a confession. I didn't really come for the salmon."

David grabbed Jules' hand and pulled her down the hallway to his bedroom. Even though his parents wouldn't be home for a week, he closed the door and locked it. Just in case. Her hands lightly scraped across his stomach, and he felt a rush of nerves tingle throughout his body. They kissed long and hard, twisting and dipping their tongues into each other's mouths. He pushed her slowly onto the bed and she allowed it with a natural fluidity. His hips began to grind with hers. She panted softly and David watched her cheeks turn blush-red. After a few minutes of kissing her on the mouth he switched to her ear. This made her moan softly. He was beginning to feel a familiar urge that he'd felt many times before, but never as strong as it was now. David began caressing her body with his fingers, tracing her contours.

"Do you have it? The condom," she whispered softly into his ear. Then she lowered the straps of her shirt down, exposing her black bra. Her hands disappeared behind her back, and she let her bra fall to the side of the bed. "This feels right, David."

David removed his shirt. He didn't like his body. He wasn't fat or hairy, but he was very skinny and the bones in his back and shoulders stuck out. He looked to his dresser drawer and frowned. He knew that he'd forgotten something and now his stomach churned. "I don't. Damn it." He hammered his fist against the bed mattress.

"Ooohhh, David, are you sure?" she asked while lightly scratching his back. Then she sat up and let out a deep breath, turned to him and rested her hand on his shoulders. "Maybe this wasn't meant to be. It's okay, David."

"I'm really sorry. I know what might help," he said as his confidence returned. His head lowered and he kissed her breasts and continued down to her navel. His fingers fumbled with the button of her jean shorts. She smelled of perfume and her skin was soft and tan. His tongue made circular motions above her navel. She pulled him back up. Her face was still red as she shook it.

"Come here," she said as she waved him forward.

He moved forward and they held each other. He kissed her shoulder and her skin felt warm.

She began to breathe heavy. They started kissing. She ran her fingers down his bare back.

"Tell me this is right."

"But I don't have a . . . I'm so sorry," he said.

"If this is meant to be, it will be okay."

"I won't . . . you know . . . inside you," he said, laying her down.

3

She squeezed the skin on his back and stopped moving.

"Go slow. This is my first time," she said. "I can't believe we're doing this."

David slowed down until her hips began moving with his again. A tinge of guilt dwelled within her, and her heart was not entirely into what they were doing. But she wanted this, and it meant that their relationship was growing. Afterward, they rolled onto their backs and held each other.

They were silent for a long moment.

"It didn't hurt that bad," Jules told him.

"That was amazing, Jules."

She smiled, happy to please him. Jules' eyelids dipped and she readjusted against his chest. A little nap was in order, and afterward they could hang out, watch a movie and relax. Enjoy the new level of their relationship.

4

David liked being inside of her. There had been only two sexual experiences for him in the past and they had ended with him prematurely ejaculating. This time was better than anything he'd ever felt before and he wanted more. He lightly nudged her arm and ran his fingers around her navel.

"I don't know if I can do it again," Jules said, rolling onto her side.

"Like never?" David asked, wondering if he'd done something wrong within the last few minutes that they'd been lying here.

"No, I mean I'm sore. We can do this again when the time is right."

He wondered when that could be, but right now he felt good about being with Jules. Not just sexually. Everything about her was wonderful and now he just wanted to lie with her. Be with her.

Chapter 5

Ted's Desire grows

1

Ted Olson traveled down Briar Road and connected with County Trunk A on his way into Watertown. He needed to restock at the grocery store. Red meat, pickled herring, eggs, bacon, and white bread were at the top of his short list. Ted didn't care about eating fancy, he only needed nourishment. His appetite was for something more than delicious foods and home cooked meals. It had been over two months since his last kill, and he needed to hunt again. He'd found the last score at a park forty miles north of Watertown in Middletown, a fair-sized suburb of Madison.

The blonde-haired girl had been all alone as she walked through the parking lot, making it easy for Ted to sneak up behind her and knock her unconscious with the grip of his .44 Bulldog. When she woke up in his barn naked and tied to the bumper of his old broken-down Chevy, which had been collecting rust since it stopped running over a decade ago, he had taunted her for a few hours then untied her after midnight. She'd been one of the few who'd run toward the woods. Usually, his scores ran for the road, with the assumption that someone might drive past and help. In the past year or so, Ted had seen only two cars drive by. There was nothing out here—except for Ted. And that was the way he liked it.

The girl sprinted about fifty yards before Ted slung his hatchet at her. It hit low and clipped her ankles out from beneath her. Her head slammed onto the ground.

Jumping on her first, straddling her, he slammed his fists onto the back of her head, then he dismembered her with the hatchet.

She became another, of many, to be buried in the field behind the barn. Ted didn't do things with her head the way he had done things with some of the others.

2

The bright fluorescent lights that filled the grocery store annoyed Ted and gave him a headache. He was a night person and the light made him feel vulnerable and exposed. The light didn't allow him to go undetected. People could see him in the light. He filled his grocery cart with eighteen packages of bacon, a few cartons of eggs, and everything else that he wanted. The checkout clerk was a young beauty with brunette hair. She would make a fine score, but it wouldn't be quite as fulfilling as a blonde.

"You sure like bacon," the girl said.

Ted assumed that she was trying to make conversation. He didn't respond to her.

3

Ted made a detour on his way back home. First, he drove through the downtown area of Watertown and watched all the weaker beings as they moped down the sidewalks and looked into the shop windows. They were weak and he was strong, but some days he wished that he could be more like them. Life would be much simpler. He could have married and maybe had children. Watched them grow up. He could have retired with a woman that he loved. Love: a word that he wished he understood. It had been thrown around throughout his life; at school, at work, but never at home. Never had Ted's mother told him that she loved him. She'd said that to say it was to tell a lie—that it was something that people felt, not said. People made the word up so they could justify their inability to survive and compete on their own. Ted knew better than to love. Love was the act of pretending to be sympathetic to the needs of others. These simple people had to lie to themselves to get through their days, their lives. Ted was better than them—he was strong, and he was better. He turned onto Interstate 94 and drove out of town toward the Jefferson House.

He parked in the empty lot near the back entrance. He'd sat there many times before. The place looked the same, the wood was rotting, and the paint was peeling badly, yet it was still open for business. In fact, there was a banner hanging over the front door that read "Spring Formal Welcome Seniors." It must be a dance.

A hunt.

There would be plenty of scores to choose from if he could make it out here undetected. He'd only hunted here once before, and that was twenty-nine years ago. He'd taken a young couple. He'd quickly killed the boy, but the girl had been his best score. He'd even used her head for several days afterward.

The hairs on the back of Ted's neck stood tall and he found himself gripping the steering wheel tight.

This dance would suffice for a good, well planned, hunt.

He drove up close to the banner and read that the dance was coming up in just over a month. His truck spun out in the gravel, and he was off onto Briar Road, headed toward home.

Hunger growled through his stomach, and he craved bacon.

4

It was well after nine o'clock and Ted's belly was full. He wasn't tired. He was revved up and wanted to hunt. The sensations he felt were not going to go away. They never did. Maybe if he went out and cruised, he would become settled. That is what he would do. In the towns surrounding Madison, he could find a small bar and stop in for a drink. He was an old hermit, not a young, strapping boy, and Madison was the very definition of a college town. He'd be out of place and that was unacceptable. But towns like Sun Prairie and Middleton would allow him to blend in. The taverns and bars that catered to these towns serviced the young and old alike.

Staring in the mirror at his reflection, he digested his aged face. His skin was tanned with liver spots, which looked like large freckles. His jaw muscles were strong and punched out at the corners of his square, masculine face. His cheeks were sunken in, and his cold eyes flickered in the bathroom light. The gray hair that fell from his scalp looked silver now. He placed his forty-year-old Milwaukee Brewers cap on his head and left the bathroom, flipping the light switch off as he left, to save money on the electric bill.

5

The night was silent, and he drove with the windows rolled down, the breeze cooling his warm face. The excitement had boiled his blood and his cheeks felt flush and hot.

He slowed down as he entered Sun Prairie town limits. Driving down Main Street he saw the neon lights of local taverns. At the far end of the street, near the edge of town, he found the bar that had called to him on this night. He parked in back, far enough away from the crowded part of the parking lot. His tan work-boots settled on the blacktop, and he walked to the rear entrance of the bar.

The building was old, wooden, and painted brown. Even in the dark, Ted could see that it could use a fresh coat of paint. In the light it probably looked worse. The cigarette smoke in the bar clouded his sense of smell and he found a small table in the back. He ordered a beer from the bartender and went back to the table and sipped from his soap spotted glass. About fifteen patrons sat at the bar, most of which had migrated near the large flat screen television that showed a basketball game. Country music played at a good volume from the juke box near the entrance. The front door opened, and the blonde girl entered. She was a little pudgy, but she had a very attractive face. She smiled at the bartender, then went to the counter and took a drink that had been made for her in a small clear glass. A lime sat on top of the ice and Ted assumed that it was a gin and tonic. The woman was alone. She talked briefly with the bartender and sipped her drink. Ted ordered another beer, drank it, then left the tavern undetected. The girl would suffice.

Ted moved his van across the parking lot next to a crowd of trees with draping vines. In the dark, the van was barely visible.

He pulled the stereo out from its slot, set it on the passenger's seat, then dug into the empty slot and retrieved his .44 Bulldog revolver. He stuck it in his boot and covered it with his denim jeans. He stepped out into the night and waited beyond the parking lot near a cluster of trees.

Patiently waiting, at a little after midnight, the young blond left the bar and walked down the sidewalk, stumbling slightly.

Even better, she walked.

Ted followed her silently. She stopped in front of a small brick home and stumbled down the walkway. Excitedly, Ted rushed her as she pulled her keys from her purse. His hand wrapped around her mouth, then he reached down and grabbed the revolver. He slammed it into the side of her face and caught her as she slumped to the ground.

He dragged her through the back lawns of the small houses that lined the street at the edge of town. Swiftly, he placed her in the van and zip tied her hands and feet. With hemp rope, he gagged her mouth closed. Heart beating fast, Ted hopped into the van and drove home.

The ride went quick, and after only half an hour he was parked at his barn. With shaky hands, he walked into the barn, grabbed his freshly sharpened axe from the back wall and went to the van. Breathing deeply, he opened the sliding side door. Behind her gag, the girl screamed, but it sounded more like a moan. Her mascara was dripping down both sides of her face and her white shirt was wet from perspiration. Grabbing her beautiful blond hair, Ted yanked her from the van and watched her slam onto the gravel driveway. With his axe, he lightly traced her back while she crawled away like a large caterpillar. Smiling, he raised the axe high and slammed it down between her feet, severing the zip ties and allowing the score to stand and make a run for it.

When she stood, Ted noticed that he had sliced off a good piece of her calf while releasing her. Disregarding her wound, she sprinted down the driveway. Her hands were still tied behind her back. They bumped her lower back repeatedly as she ran away from Ted. She didn't look back until she reached the entrance of the driveway. And when she did, she met the cold steel edge of Ted's axe as it slammed into her face, slicing the rope that gagged her, splitting deep into her mouth. Bloody mist erupted from her head and Ted's second chop hammered her to the ground. His body shivered with delight as his score withered and flopped across the ground. His next chop took her arm off at the elbow and she screamed loud and guttural into the chilly night. Ted howled with delight, then bent down and picked up her arm. The weight of it was empowering and he went to her and tore off her clothes.

Naked, bleeding, and screaming from a broken face, the girl still fought to get away. Ted undressed. When he was completely naked, he lowered himself onto her. She flailed as he took her and when he was finished, he stood and slung his axe into her one last time. Her head rolled to the side, and she stopped movement all together.

Before the sun rose in the morning, the blond score was in ten separate pieces. Blood drenched the gravel drive and led to the field where Ted carried the pieces to the small hole he'd dug, twenty yards into his property. The smell of her burning flesh was a pleasure in the romantic sunrise of the new day. Her head sat next to the hole. Ted wasn't sure if he wanted to keep it or not.

Chapter 6
Cravings

1

Jules Benton was glowing, she felt new, rejuvenated. She stared at her reflection in the bathroom mirror. Her skin appeared radiant, her hair silky and straight. Not a strand out of place. Looking at herself, she was reminded of a hair salon commercial. One in which the sexy actress shakes her head in slow motion and her hair shines as if each long strand was a string of silk.

Then, sweet thoughts of David swam into her head, and she felt the thin white hairs on her arm lift and rise from her skin. The recurring fantasy of her and David attending college together floated dizzily at the forefront of her mind. Maybe, after graduation he would propose, they could have children. They would live in town— here—and raise a family. It was simple. It was heaven.

Lowering her head, she put a halt to the spiraling infinity of her daydreams. She inhaled a full breath of air. Exhaling and quickly inhaling again, her chest rose, and she admired the look that her new bra provided. It was supposed to make her breasts appear more voluptuous, bigger, and sexier. It had done the trick. It felt awkward, like her breasts were being scrunched together like tomatoes in a mesh bag. It didn't hurt, but it more or less felt like she was wearing a harness.

But if David liked it, then the bra was okay.

The spring formal was coming up in about a month. She and David needed to finalize their plans. They still didn't know if they were going to join Penny and Mark or if they wanted to go by themselves. Either or, it would be a great night.

David had officially asked Jules to attend the dance with him months ago. And of course she'd said yes. How could she not? It would be the best date—for a dance—that she'd ever had. So much had happened since the night that he'd asked her. Wow, it had already been three weeks since they'd made love for the first time.

Jules' train of thought broke when her father's heavy fist began rapping at the bathroom door.

"Hey sweetie, how long are you gonna be?" Richard asked.

"Almost done, dad," she returned.

"Your mom is using our bathroom and I have to go number two—tacos for lunch," he explained.

The thought of her dad's bowel movements containing tacos shot Jules out of her daydream. Almost gagging, she rolled her eyes and pulled the long sleeves of her white cotton shirt over her head and straightened the V-neck so that the V was directly aligned with the crease of her cleavage. Nodding approvingly with her appearance, she twisted the doorknob and opened the door. Quickly, she slid past her father. Never in her life had Jules witnessed her father's head turn so fast. For a moment, she thought that he'd hurt his neck. Trying her best to ignore the judging look on his face, Jules was certain that he'd noticed how revealed her breasts were.

"All yours, dad." She darted into her room, her voice still in the air while she was pulling the door shut.

She found her cell phone on the dresser, picked it up, and punched in David's phone number. His greeting came quick, after only one ring.

Jules melted with appreciation.

"Good morning to you," Jules said.

"Good morning back. What do you think about going to Tim Butner's house tonight? He's having a kegger."

"That sounds good. I have to be home before midnight though, or my dad will flip out," Jules shamefully admitted. Most of her friends were free of curfew. Also, she knew that her dad didn't care much for David. The few times she'd invited David home for dinner, he'd pummeled him with embarrassing questions. *Where are you taking my daughter? What time are you going to have her back?* And she hated it when he referred to her as *my daughter.* She was parked right in front of him and yet he talked to David as though she were a million miles away. Plus, she'd already addressed the night's logistics with her father, prior to

David's arrival. His disregard for her feelings displayed a lack of trust and respect.

"I'll get you home before midnight. No problem," David finally answered.

"Good. I'll see you at school then."

"Later," David returned before ending the call.

Later.

Late.

I'm late!

A blinding realization occurred to Jules. She was late for her period. There had only been a handful of missed menstrual cycles in the past. The fact was: there were at least three times. The difference between *then* and *now* was that she wasn't sexually active *then*.

David hadn't worn a condom.

Immediately, panic seized Jules' thoughts.

It's okay. You've been late before.

She was paranoid with good reason. It could be shaken off—for now—because she wasn't going to let paranoia ruin her Friday night.

2

Penny picked Jules up for school at seven-thirty on the dot. The day zipped by. Her boring classroom activities flew on as visions of David ravaging her danced in her imagination. From algebra to American History, the day blasted past with nothing retained but fantastic thoughts of her current love.

Jules invited Penny to attend the party with her and *her man.* Penny agreed, eager to tag along, although in the past she'd hated being attached as the third wheel. Since the moment Jules vividly relayed her sexual experiences with David to Penny, she seemed to be overly interested in the goings-on between the two. Jules didn't dwell upon it much at the time, but she'd experienced moments where she thought that Penny had a little crush on David. She was always smiling at him with her pouty little peepers as if she was in on the secret to their relationship. It was chalked up to a slight case of paranoia. And even if Penny did have a crush, that was alright. Sometimes it was enlightening to know that others were enamored by the one you were with.

Spring was just around the corner and the Midwestern winter was really starting to ease up. Perhaps it will be warm at the bonfire tonight. And perhaps Jules could wear a certain short skirt that she'd purchased on clearance sale earlier in the week. It could be deemed appropriate, she thought. Sure, she secretly fantasized about what David could do to her at the party if she wore a short skirt. It would provide him with easier access. Thoughts of David pulling her away from the party, into a private spot, maybe behind the barn, made the hair on the back of her neck tingle. She had to hold back a smile. Her legs trembled. Holding back laughter now—silly girl—she had to place a hand over her knee to keep it from bumping up and down against her desk.

3

Shuttling Jules home from school, Penny began to wonder why Jules had such a bad case of the giggles. They hadn't spoken more than ten words to each other since they hopped in the car. And what they'd spoken of wasn't all that funny. She was sure of it.

The rest of the drive home was silent, and Penny never asked what Jules' deal was. Arriving in the Benton's driveway, Jules sat up, leaned across the seat, and hugged Penny without making a peep. *No goodbye? No see you later?*

Stars and glitter were showering all over Jules' world and Penny wanted in on the fun.

"I'll see you tonight, then?" Penny spoke up, but Jules was already halfway up the driveway.

"Yeah, pick me up at seven, then we'll swing by David's house," Jules said.

"Sure thing. Till then."

Penny watched as Jules disappeared into the house.

What to wear tonight? Penny thought while she sped home to relax a little before the party.

4

At six o'clock, Jules hopped in the shower and washed up. The spray of hot water trickled down her face, stomach, and curved between her *privates,* barely touching the sensitive skin between her legs. The urge to *touch* presented itself.

No.

David would be with her, later. She would save her excitement for him.

By six twenty-five, Jules was dolled-up in a short skirt with a thin white cotton shirt, covered with a light jacket. Walking out from the bathroom, Richard took one look at Jules, halted her, and blocked her path before she could make an escape into the solitude of her bedroom.

"What are you wearing?" he asked.

"Clothes, daddy. What does it look like I'm wearing?" she whimpered.

"It looks like you're not wearing enough. Go put something … less revealing on." He was calm but demanding.

Plans of seducing David with her sexy skirt were being foiled with each passing moment and Jules knew that if she persisted, she would only lose the battle and possibly be prevented from going out at all. Her bottom lip curled, and her eyebrows scrunched low above the top of her nose. Her last defense would be to guilt him.

"But daddy, everybody wears this kind of stuff."

"Yeah, well not you. Go change." He clapped his hands together—once—signifying that he wanted her to jump on it, now.

Her shoulders slumped and she groaned while pushing her bedroom door open.

Ruffling through her wardrobe, Jules became agitated. She thought about wearing her cute blue sundress but then realized that it would be too light. She'd freeze all over, at least with a short skirt, only her legs would feel the cold air. The sundress was for summer. A long denim skirt that stopped below the knees became the object of compromise. It was modest but provided easier access than jeans. Plus, it matched the rest of her outfit.

She peeled her skirt off and tossed it on the ground behind her bed. Pulling the long denim skirt up over her white thong, she turned, glanced at her tight behind in the mirror, and thought *not bad*. And with that, her excitement was restored. She winked in the mirror, then shuffled out of her room. In the living room, Richard and Mary watched *Wheel of Fortune*. This had been their favorite game show for years, watching it on the couch with a snack had become a ritual of sorts. Richard was the first to notice Jules walking down the hallway when he turned his head to stuff a handful of butter-free popcorn in his mouth. Standing quickly, he went to Jules and intercepted her as she headed into the kitchen.

Richard pulled a bottle of beer from the fridge and twisted the cap off. A faint hiss escaped the bottle as the carbonation fizzed with oxygen. He took down a hefty chug and shook his head.

He settled.

"Look, I know you want to look pretty for that boyfriend of yours . . . I understand that. When I was in high school I wanted to look good for all of my dates too. It's just . . . hard . . . for me to look at you like this because I still see my little baby girl . . ."

"But dad . . ." Jules chimed in.

Richard held up his hand, index finger extended. "Let me finish. I can see your underwear when you wear those short skirts honey . . . and I know how boys are. I don't want you running into a situation where you get taken advantage of . . . for any reason . . . even dressing in those skimpy clothes can get you in trouble. I know you think that I'm being ridiculous, but I'm doing it because I care."

Jules watched her father morph from a disciplinarian into what looked like a sad little boy. Her stomach dropped like a ton of ice, and she couldn't help but to hold him. They embraced each other tight.

"I understand daddy, but soon I won't be your little girl anymore. I'm going to be your grown-up daughter—a woman," Jules explained.

"You want to bet?"

She felt the hot sting of tears rushing up the back of her throat. Penny's horn honked obnoxiously in the driveway.

"Maybe you should keep your eyes open for other boys too, Jules."

At this, she only frowned, then scurried out the front door. "Bye mom!" she shouted.

"Have fun," Mary hollered back.

Quickly as she left the house, Jules could feel her face become warm as blood rushed through her body and into her face, filling the capillaries beneath her radiant skin. She was excited to see David, wanted to feel his touch. Every moment that she wasn't with him, she was obsessing over him. About the way he would touch her and how he would make her tingle inside. *Only David*. The way his soft lips felt when she kissed him. Only David could do that to her. She smiled when she remembered how self-conscious he'd become when she observed him shirtless for the first time. He didn't need to be. To her, he was perfect. He was all that she would ever need. Jules jumped into the car, closed the door and eyed up Penny. Making sure she wasn't dressed too similar. It had happened before.

Penny wore a white cotton skirt that matched her black halter-top. She had on more make-up than usual, which Jules thought odd, but didn't say anything. The eyeshadow gave a weird goth-vibe that she probably didn't intend on.

Once on the road, they zipped down the well-lit residential street. Jules caught a glimpse of her father while he stood in the living room window, waving goodbye. She smiled and waved back, knowing that he couldn't see her.

The sweet sting of Penny's Marlboro cigarette caught Jules' attention when it weaved through the air and found her sense of smell.

"You look hot tonight!" Penny barked as smoke escaped her mouth, making her look oddly demonic. Her smile looked strange, and it seemed too big for her face. Jules couldn't help but to think that maybe Penny was dressed to impress David. Even though she would never hurt Jules like that, she knew that Penny liked it when Jules' boyfriends gawked at her.

"Thanks Penny, I really like your outfit too," Jules returned while she reevaluated Penny's garb. Her legs were glimmering like she'd used some kind of rejuvenating lotion containing sparkles.

Penny dug into her purse and retrieved a small plastic bottle of chardonnay. She handed it to Jules and retrieved another. "A little pre-party cocktail? I picked up a four pack."

Jules took the bottle, twisted the top off and downed a sip. It was warm and didn't go down very smoothly. She didn't really feel like drinking, but she didn't want to make Penny feel guilty or alone either. The sting of alcohol seeped into her blood stream, and she felt a sense of calm followed by more thoughts of David. These images were more risqué than before. Earlier in the day, she thought about the feelings that David induced within her, a different kind of arousal. Now she was thinking about dirty things. Things that she wanted him to do to her tonight. Things like putting him in her mouth. Normally, she didn't think about acts such as these, but the mood seemed right, and she *wanted* to think about these things. Forget guilt and morality, not tonight. She couldn't help but *want* to think about animalistic-carnal-acts.

Another sip of wine settled her nerves.

When they pulled into David's driveway, Jules immediately locked her eyes on him. He was waiting underneath the garage door. Again, her nerves swam rambunctiously when he looked at her. His blue jeans and black tee shirt gave him a bad-boy look. She liked it. She watched as his lips parted and a boyish smile formed across his mouth. Hopefully, he was happy to see her. She saw that Penny had an identical smile set upon her face. Jules' nerves turned fiery. David hopped in the car, leaned over the passenger seat and kissed Jules. It was a sweet kiss on the corner of her mouth. Her anger was gone.

"You guys both look great tonight. Especially you, Jules," David said as he ran his index finger down the side of Jules' face.

His finger tickled. It made her shiver. Her wild thoughts fumbled crazily, making her dizzy. She turned to look at him, and he planted another kiss on her, this time on the lips. From the corners of her mouth, she felt a twittering sensation. Butterflies flipped through her belly.

"You guys are too much," Penny called out while she stared at David in the rear-view mirror. Penny looked animalistic, her teeth jutted out in front of her lips, and she was batting her eyes at him. Jules thought she looked, strangely, like the wolf from "Little Red Riding Hood."

A ten-minute drive later, they arrived at the party. In unison, the three of them popped out of the car and stood on the gravel driveway, which lead to a dirt path through the backyard. The bonfire danced in the dark night about a hundred yards down from where they'd parked.

The brisk night air felt icy, and Jules was shivering. David took his jacket off and wrapped it around her shoulders.

"Can I have your shirt?" Penny joked.

Jules found no humor in her comments—this time—and she sent Penny a hairy eye. Penny's grin flipped to a scowl. "What?" she barked.

"Nothing," Jules returned. She dropped it, not wanting to look insecure in front of Penny or David.

David shook his head and chuckled.

Penny and Jules both tripped on their walk down to the bonfire. Their heels were sinking into the ground with each step.

The fire crackled loud in the clear night and the shouts of over forty teenagers echoed across the green landscape of the farm. As they approached the fire, a few friends stumbled past and said hello, inquired about school, the party, and social gossip.

Jules was already scoping the area, making a mental note of any hideaway spots for her and David to escape to later on, maybe after a few beers. No one would notice they were gone.

When Penny, Jules, and David finally landed in the main crowd, the hooting and hollering became quiet, probably so the party-people could stop and inspect the newcomers. Jules liked this part. It made her feel like the guest of honor, if only for half of a second. David kissed the top of her head.

"You want a beer?" David asked.

"Yes, please."

"Oh, can you grab me one too?" Penny chimed in. "If you see a foo-foo drink . . . that'd be even better, thanks."

David looked from Jules to Penny and grinned. "Sure thing." He walked off toward the keg, which sat in a large plastic bucket full of ice, up the trail.

"What was that . . . before?" Penny asked.

"What was what?" Jules returned.

"You got all cranky when I asked David for his shirt. I was kidding."

"I thought it was a little inappropriate."

Penny tilted her head back and chuckled. Her hands shot out at Jules' side and tickled her. "You are a jealous girl. I think you might be in l-o-v-e."

Jules began to blush, and she cuddled in next to Penny and rested her head on her shoulder. "I am . . . I'm sorry . . . Do you hate me?"

"Of course not. However, if you guys want to have a threesome later . . . I think I'd be down. David is hot."

Jules popped away from Penny. She felt rage come over her again then realized that Penny was joking. Embarrassed, she shook her head. "I'm such an idiot."

David came back, holding two red plastic cups in his right hand and one in his left. He gave one to Jules, the other to Penny then raised his cup. All three of them clanked plastic.

"Cheers." He put the cup to his lips then turned to Penny and said, "Sorry, they didn't have any foo-foo drinks." Penny shrugged her shoulders and chugged. "I'm gonna mingle. Mark is gone fishing for the weekend with his dad," Penny explained before she bounced off toward a group of boys standing near a messy stack of wooden pallets. Two of the boys, wearing letter jackets, were pulling one of the pallets off the pile and heaving it above their heads, about to throw it on the fire, which must have been six feet high already.

They chucked it.

Jules and David watched on as Penny dodged sparks when the wood landed on the fire.

David and Jules laughed at her while she hollered at the boys who'd tossed the pallet onto the fire. Jules rubbed her arms and chattered her teeth. She tilted her face to David.

"You want to go for a walk and check the place out?"

A bit slow, it took a moment for David to catch the hook, but then he raised his eyebrows and repeated her question. "Go for a walk?"

Realizing that she wanted to fool around, he eagerly grabbed her hand and dragged her off toward the barn, a few hundred feet from the party.

Along the way, they saw other boys and girls making out, hiding from the main gathering. Jules wanted something even more secluded than this. She wanted to do more with David than just make-out. The excitement of what they could do was making her hot. Despite the cold, she could feel her forehead begin to perspire.

They skirted around to the backside of the barn where the noises from the party were muffled and distant. Back here, there were no more stragglers from the party. Jules pulled David toward a pile of hay bales. She pushed him against the highest stack and kissed him. Wiggling between his legs, she could no longer control herself. David's hands dipped under her shirt, massaging her breasts. Jules' breath was fast and hard. David kissed her ears, and it was driving her crazy. Her hands ran down the back of his shirt, grabbing at his butt cheeks and squeezing them. He wasn't muscular but she liked the feel of his warm skin. Her right hand slid across his stomach; she felt his gooseflesh. She dipped her hand down the front of his pants. His belt was tight, and she had to squeeze her hand below his waistband.

David smiled down at her. "Your hand is cold."

Jules immediately retracted her hand from his body. Shaking his head, he quickly grabbed her wrist and pushed her hand back. "It feels great though."

Jules was relieved. Again, she grabbed him. David's breath was heavy, his fingertips fiddled between her thighs, and they danced around the edge of her cotton thong. She began to moan. A short while later, she parted from him and calculated the distance between them and the party, a smile forming on her face.

"You want to?" Jules asked.

"Here? Now?"

Jules only bobbed her head up and down, slowly. David looked back from the party to Jules, and he mimicked her, bobbing his head up and down. David took his coat from around Jules' shoulders and laid it out on the bale of hay near the barn. Jules moved up to it and she kicked her leg up and rested her foot on the hay. She bent over and pulled up her skirt. She felt vulnerable, but it was exciting. It wasn't degrading because David respected her. She allowed her inhibitions to diminish, then she heard his zipper go down, and felt him entering her.

It ended quickly.

"Was . . . was that okay?" David asked.

It was too fast, but Jules liked the idea of *being dirty* and she didn't want him to feel bad. Plus, even though it was fast and animalistic, it was exciting to do something that she had never done before.

Naughty.

He was quick, but overall, it was pleasurable. It didn't hurt like the first time, which wasn't all that bad either. Yet, all the same, she couldn't help but feel the cold surge of guilt expand in the pit of her stomach. And was the experience only good in her fantasy or was the act in itself fulfilling? Jules thought the latter, but still felt a yearning to be intimate with David.

The night air rushed over her half-exposed body and so did her guilt. Everything she had ever been taught by her father, teachers, and pastor had been thrown out into the wind. She couldn't help looking up at the sky. The moon was full, a gathering of dark gray clouds passed by, making it appear yellow.

God was angry.

Again, he hadn't worn a condom.

Though her feelings for David had peaked, she couldn't face him. Her morality had been compromised; thoughts ran through her mind of the talks she had with her mother about sex.

Her mother had sat her down once, when she was very young, and explained that she wanted to talk about the birds and the bees. Young and naïve, Jules thought her mom wanted to talk about the garden out back because a new wasp nest showed up above the shed near the green beans. When her mother said the word "penis" Jules had become mortified. She knew what one was—she'd seen her dad's once after he walked out of the shower. He didn't know that she was there.

She was ashamed to think of that now.

Mom wanted Jules to wait for the right person.

"I know that you probably won't wait until after you're married, sweetie, but I hope that you can wait until you're in love . . . and you know that he loves you back . . . truly," she'd explained.

"Did you wait until you were married?" Jules had asked her mother.

Jules remembered that her mother had looked away. It was the first time that Jules could remember seeing her ashamed. "I didn't, no . . . and that's why I'm telling you . . . now . . . to wait. If I thought that what I did was right . . . then I wouldn't be telling you to wait. I didn't love the first man I had . . . times . . . with. He was wrong and

I was wrong, and I felt used . . . for a long time. It made the world around me change and I thought less of myself. Then I met your father and all that changed because he thought the world of me. He cared about me, and I loved the way he made me feel about myself. Does any of this make sense to you, Jules?"

Jules had been relieved when she looked up from her lap to see that her mother was smiling again. Talking about the way her dad made her feel cheered her spirit. Seeing her mother's affection for her father was inspiring.

"I'll wait until I find a boy that loves me," Jules promised before she lunged forward and latched onto her mother.

Now, standing behind the barn at a keg party, Jules wanted to cry. She wanted to take back her virginity and wait. She wondered if she truly loved David or if she just loved the idea of having such intense feelings for him. Guilty and cold, Jules walked along the dirt path back toward the hollers, laughs, and fire where her friends were. She'd walked alone for almost twenty yards before realizing that she'd left David back near the hay bales.

"Wait up!" David was yelling out to her while he stumbled along the path, pulling his belt tight. He cupped his hands around her shoulders when he caught up to her and pulled her back, stopping her from moving forward. She tried to shrug him off. "What's the matter?"

Jules turned to him with cold eyes and stared deep into his face. "Do you love me?"

David took a step back. He looked like a deer stuck in headlights. Even in the dark, Jules could see that he was blushing and uncomfortable. "Slow down Jules, talk to me. What's wrong?"

"Are we *really* ready for this? Sex. Because if we are . . . then I want to know why I feel so crappy right now," Jules responded.

"Jules, we talked about this, and we both agreed that we were ready."

"I think I was wrong," Jules said, folding her arms across her chest.

"Well, I wasn't the one who initiated what happened back there, Jules. In case you forgot, you were the one who dragged me back there . . . and you were the one who grabbed me, pulled your skirt up, and let me fuck you," David said with dark intensity.

Jules was afraid now, and she felt guilty. Not only for giving herself to this boy, but for forcing her guilt onto him afterward. "You're right. I'm sorry, I just feel kind of dirty."

"Jules, if you don't want to do this, then don't seduce me. I think . . . I thought we were ready, and I would have waited if you had wanted to . . . but you didn't. You wanted to have sex, and so did I and I don't regret it. Do I love you . . . I think I do, but I wanted to wait until I was absolutely sure before I told you."

David's last words made Jules want to grab him and hold him tight. But she could tell that he was too upset, and not in the mood anymore. His shoulders slumped and he pulled her into him and held her.

"I understand. Let's hold off on the sex for a while, okay?"

And in that moment, Jules felt that her guilt may have been misguided. Maybe they were *ready* for sex, and she was just feeling a little guilt because it was all so new. Right now, she just wanted to relish in the moment and feel good about holding David.

After a few beers and a couple of laughs, Jules needed to get home. She nudged David and rolled her eyes. Not at David, but for causing an inconvenience while they drove her home.

Penny wasn't nearly as drunk as Jules had thought she'd be, and she was quick to separate herself from the social gatherings of the party.

Surprising but logical, Penny dropped Jules off first and allowed for a few good night kisses in the driveway before taking David home. Jules didn't like the idea of Penny and David driving home together, but in the end, she didn't have a choice. What would he do, walk home? Also, she was being paranoid again. She watched anxiously while David's lips curled into a smile and gave her one final kiss before driving off with Penny.

Jules turned and looked at the house for a moment before creeping up the driveway and entering through the garage. She didn't want to wake up her parents. Not now, after what she'd done. Hoping that her father hadn't watched her making out with David in the driveway, she snuck into the kitchen. As it was, her parents weren't awake, and Jules quickly slipped down the hallway and slid into her bedroom.

She pulled her diary from under the mattress and aimed her silver reading lamp directly onto the neatly bound leather journal that her grandmother had given her last Christmas before she died. She had only started writing in it a few months ago. About the time she started dating David. She grabbed an ink pen and began scribbling.

With pleasant thoughts, she slept well.

5

Penny watched David while he stared out the passenger side window of the car. She wanted to touch him, even though it would ruin her relationship with Jules, if she ever found out.

She couldn't help herself.

"So, what were you and Jules doing behind the barn tonight?" Penny asked, not really wanting an answer, but wanting to bring up the topic of sex.

David chuckled and turned toward Penny. "What?"

"You guys fuck a lot?" Penny asked. She could feel her stomach begin to tingle with a warm sensation. She kept a straight face. "I'm just teasing you, David," she said, then grabbed the upper part of his thigh.

David's face was turning red. Penny smiled seductively; she'd gotten to him. She traced the outline of his body with eager eyes, sure that he could read her thoughts.

"Do you want to go back to the party?" Penny asked.

"Sure, I guess," David responded. "I mean I don't want to piss Jules off or anything."

"We could go somewhere else if you wanted. We could go out to The Garden out on Highway 26," Penny said, knowing full-well that The Garden was a hotspot for heavy make-out sessions. She wanted to feel David out. See how loyal he was to *his woman.*

Penny was certain that David was confused. He was staring at her with wide eyes while his mouth quivered. Given the intensity of his face, she didn't know if he was smiling or frowning. "Are you serious?"

"I don't know. Am I?" She reached over and grabbed his thigh again. This time, she grabbed very high on his leg, near his groin, and she could tell that he was becoming erect. His jeans had lifted near the zipper.

"I guess we could, I mean if you wanted to."

"Yeah, it's pretty out there this time of night."

6

The highway turned into a one-way dirt road that disappeared into the woods. Penny flipped on the high beams, illuminating a bend in the road that curled around a small pond in the middle of The Garden Wildlife Reserve.

When they finally parked, Penny turned the headlights off and turned to David.

Everything was dark.

Everything was silent.

"It's no big deal. She's not going to find out if we don't tell her." Penny leaned over and kissed him.

She tried to push her tongue into his mouth, but he wouldn't allow it. He pulled away from her.

"We can't do this to Jules. I'm into her . . . no joke," David said. But he leaned toward her, stopping an inch in front of her face. Her stomach was flipping over and over, she wanted him badly. They could hop in the back seat, and he could take her there, if he wanted to.

"If we can't do this," she mimicked him, "Why didn't you stop us from coming here?" Penny asked anxiously.

He turned away and looked out the window, licking his lips. "Are you sure no one will find out? I mean you're Jules' best friend. If she finds out, both of us are in trouble."

"I think that if you just be a man and have sex with me . . . and neither of us says anything . . . then we'll be fine . . . like it never happened. We can have fun. It's not like we're killing anyone."

"You're okay with that?"

She grabbed his crotch, unzipped his jeans for him, and he slid them all the way off.

After a short while, they were in the back seat. Penny felt a rush of guilt, but she was too turned on to stop. He struggled to enter her, but once he was inside, she felt her nerves fray with ecstasy. It didn't take long for her to climax and David was quick too.

Panting and eager, David whipped his clothes back on.

Penny felt used. David wouldn't even look at her and she felt degraded.

"I had a great time too, David," she said sarcastically. She made no attempt to get dressed.

"Can you take me home?" David asked while he pulled his shirt over his head, settling in the front seat.

"Sure. Whatever," she said before leaning over and searching for her clothes.

They dressed in silence.

7

The drive home was silent. When they pulled into David's driveway, he forced a smile and nodded. He got out of the car, shuffled up the driveway, then disappeared into the house.

Penny shook her head and left. She thought about Jules and how broken-hearted she would be if she found out. She wished that she and David hadn't done what they did, but there was no taking it back now.

Would it have been that hard to just leave David alone, keep your fantasy a secret? She punched the steering wheel and shouted, "Damn it!"

She had no willpower.

This wasn't the first time she'd gone around behind Jules' back. She loved Jules—she was her best friend. But she had a knack for dating men who Penny found attractive. David wasn't the cream of the crop, but he had attributes that turned Penny on. When trying to figure out what attributes, she could only find two:

1. He was with Jules. 2. She couldn't have him.

Chapter 7
Ted's growing appetite

1

Ted Olson's truck rumbled down Briar Road near the Jefferson House. Turning his head to the side, looking at the building and the landscape surrounding it, he remembered the score he'd collected over twenty years ago. The things he'd done with her head for days afterward still aroused him. The smile that had shone brightly on the girl's face was burned into his memory. Luring the girl—and the boy—into his truck had thrilled him greatly and the memory of their frightened faces felt close. His hand slid to his groin, and he rubbed himself while he drove past the worn-out old building.

This was the third or fourth time that he'd stopped by the Jefferson House this week. There was no explanation as to why he was magnetized to the place other than to relive his morbid fantasies. He needed to be there. The excitement of being in a place where he'd hunted was enthralling. Reliving the details of the kill was orgasmic.

Ted knew he couldn't handle a hunt like that anymore. Physically, he had lost more than half of his strength and speed. His health was in decline, and he didn't like going to the doctor's office. He'd only gone to the VA Hospital in Madison a few times during the course of his life. The fact was simple: his youth had passed and he'd accepted that. Getting old hindered the physical nature of the hunt. He was almost seventy and his mind as well as his body was diminishing.

Reliving the details of his scores was satisfying though.

Stop being weak.

A grin washed over Ted's face. He imagined that a good hunt out at the Jefferson House would fill his void. One more time—if he was determined he could do it. The worst that could happen—if he were to get caught—was that he'd spend a couple years behind bars and die of old age. No biggy.

Gripping the steering wheel tight, he watched as the Jefferson House slowly disappeared in the rearview mirror. The banner for the high school dance was still hanging in front of the entrance, draped over the front door like a greeting. To Ted, the banner looked like an invitation to hunt.

Ted had retraced his hunt at the Jefferson House many times. Sometimes he would curl up in the grass and slither along the ground. Smell the earth. Feel the soil, the grass. Reenacting his scores almost seemed to turn back the hands of time. Ted took pleasure in that.

Just thinking about that girl's face, the one from the Jefferson House, while he sprang at her, made his heart hammer fast in his chest. He wanted to kill again. It hadn't been that long since his last score, but he wanted to hunt again. He needed to. Over the past three decades he'd taken too many scores to survey. Most of them were buried in the field behind his barn—his playpen. There were very few bodies that he'd left on-site and only then if it was an emergency.

Ted's last score was only a few days back and the one before that had been very unprofessional. She'd been walking through the back parking lot of a small bar—in a small town—in Iowa. After leaving the tavern, she had reached her car, pulled out a set of keys from her purse and started opening the car door. Swiftly and silently, Ted snuck up behind her and wrapped his hand around her mouth. She managed to pull his hand free, then she screamed. In hindsight, he should have let her go. Instead, he picked her up and forced her away from the parking lot. For fifty feet, she struggled vigorously until they were past the parking lot and headed near a stream. He had become winded.

Once they were on the water's edge, he tossed her toward the base of a small dam. The running water should have covered her screams. But unbeknownst to Ted, the woman's husband had left the tavern moments after she had. He must have followed his wife's screams down to the dam. Ted put his .44 Bulldog in the waistband of his pants. It would have made too much noise and drawn too much attention. He reached down to his pant leg and pulled out his eight-inch military survival knife and ripped her throat wide open. Blood gushed over his hands and the woman finally stopped screaming.

Ted took off running—hard and fast—to escape being caught. He could have killed the husband, but it would have slowed him down. Also, killing men wasn't as gratifying.

It was a sloppy kill. Ted let the excitement get to him. The woman had almost overpowered him. That woman was old and weak, and she almost escaped him. Normally he hid patiently, in silence, while he investigated his surroundings. Not this one. He'd jumped at the first sign of a thrill. It was amateur and undisciplined. He was extremely disciplined for most of his life, but the need to kill had grown unquenchable. Age had finally hindered his agility. He was in a bad spot for a hunter of his nature. For the past year he'd been visiting the locations of his previous kills. The best score that he'd ever taken was the one from the Jefferson House. He wanted to go back. He wished that he could live that night over. In years past, he wouldn't even consider killing in the same location. *Never in the same spot.*

That was a rule Ted adhered to. But now, while he pondered the strength of his discipline, he imagined that maybe twenty-nine years was long enough. It was time to come back and take another score.

But that would bring the police and another investigation.

That score had been too close to home. The closer the kills were to home, the closer he would be to getting caught.

In 1980, after the young couple went missing, there was a detective who'd stopped out to investigate him.

It was a few weeks after the disappearance. The detective tracked him down, somehow, and asked if he'd seen anything *out of the ordinary* on August 17th, the night the couple went missing. Calm as a clam, he told the detective that he had not seen anything out of the ordinary. He'd only stopped in for a beer on his way home from Milwaukee. When the detective asked what he'd been doing in Milwaukee, Ted found himself without an alibi. Shaken, he'd managed to tell the detective that he was looking for a new place to live on the south side. Said the countryside had become too isolated for him, that he was considering a move. Nothing more was said, but there was a brief moment when the detective locked a hairy eye on him, and in that moment, Ted knew that the detective was on to him.

Before the detective left, he grabbed Ted's hand and wouldn't let go. He leaned in close to Ted's ear and whispered, "Did you kill them?"

Ted's face burned red, and his throat choked up. He was sure that his hand was shaking.

The detective smiled, winked, and said, "I'm kidding. Loosen up."

Ted was paranoid for a long time after that incident. The visit had opened his eyes, and he was reluctant to hunt for some time, close to a year.

Snapping out of his trip down memory lane, he asked himself out loud, "What was the name of that detective?"

2

Ted turned into the gravel driveway of his property. The grass had grown so high that it was nearly impossible to see the house and barn; they were tucked in tight behind the greenery. Ted wasn't lazy; he just didn't want anyone finding his house.

His life was a secret and it needed to be hidden like one.

The van's engine sputtered and stopped in front of the barn. Far back, in the right corner, his old Chevy pick-up truck was parked, gathering rust. He should have gotten rid of it decades ago. He'd been driving the old white van that he'd bought from a retired electrician in town, and it proved to be a better utility vehicle than the Chevy. The van had no windows, which made it easier for him to transport his scores.

He stood in the driveway, listening to the crickets and insects buzzing and chirping in his field. In the diminishing daylight Ted found himself wondering if his *special fertilizer* had anything to do with the radiant greenness sprouting out all over his land. Even the weeds seemed a darker shade of green.

Trudging through the tall grass while he strolled across the property, he admired the small mounds where his scores were buried. The sweet smell of burning flesh seemed to be all around him. It was funny how the senses could remember things like that. The smells, the sights; he even felt an itch on his arm once when walking past a smaller mound and he remembered that it belonged to a blond score who had clawed at his arm while he removed her head with a hacksaw.

Other times, while he stood out in his yard, he thought the souls of those he'd taken may have hung around, been trapped and unable to go to their resting place. Maybe they belonged to Ted. He was their master in the afterlife. Dismissing the thought quickly, he laughed out loud. But once in a while his imagination swirled toward the fantastic. Sometimes it brought a grin to his weathered face. There was morbid pleasure in imagining that he was a collector of scores. More than anything, he thought of himself as a hunter.

He stopped walking about thirty yards beyond the barn where a slightly beaten path trailed out across his territory. He followed it to the grave of the scores he'd killed that night back in 1980.

Joan Neverman.

Ted wanted to hunt at the Jefferson House. His urge to kill was stronger than any drug, and he was addicted. While he glanced down at the mound, he visualized the two lifeless bodies burning in the hole. A sudden heaviness in his right shoulder reminded him of the weight of her head in his hand while he held it over her lifeless, burning body.

Looking out into the pink sky where the sun went down over the horizon, he removed his clothes and felt the evening wind circulating about his naked body.

"Friday, May 1st," he whispered to himself.

The banner at the Jefferson House read May 1st. He would go to this place—a dance to some, a hunting ground to Ted. He closed his eyes and felt the cold wind gently kiss his face.

Chapter 8
reality stings

1

Jules woke up Saturday morning, the last week in April, and rushed to the bathroom. She lifted the toilet seat and lurched forward. There was a deep churning in her stomach and then she heaved up last night's late-night tacos and cheap beer. Her face perspired and she felt nauseous. She was glad that her father had to work today. Normally, he only worked Monday through Friday, but once in a while the factory didn't meet the weekly production deadline and they needed Saturday to make up for it.

Jules slammed the bathroom door behind her and continued to vomit in the toilet. It was heavy, milky, and yellow, and it looked like raw eggs, not tacos. After a few heaves she felt better and went to the kitchen to grab a glass of orange juice. She could feel that her blood sugar was low, again the result of too much drinking. She had went out with David, Penny, and Mark last night. They went to Neil Benson's house. It wasn't quite a party, there were only about fifteen people there, but they made it a fun time. They played the card game "President" at the kitchen table, for the most part, and Jules had not played well. Penny played great and maintained the position of President for the majority of the evening and she was viscous. The president was the first player to be rid of all their cards, and she ordered Jules to drink after each deal as the president was allowed to do. David had just laughed at Jules while she steadily became sloppy drunk. There were a few times that Penny and David had disappeared into the backyard where they said they were smoking. Again, Jules allowed her paranoid mind to trail off into something sleazy. She imagined that Penny and David were sneaking kisses and she had to stop herself. Neither David nor Penny would do such a thing to hurt her.

After her juice and coffee, Jules put her running shorts and sneakers on and headed out the front door. She liked to run in the mornings. Usually, if she had a bit of a hangover, she would just run it out. The alcohol would drain from her pores and everything in her stomach would burn off. Then she could go home and have a nice breakfast, drink water, and hydrate.

The morning air was fresh, brisk, and refreshing to Jules. She ran at a medium pace and took her time while she trotted down Water Street and hooked a left onto Main Street. She smiled at the elderly folks who crowded the town shops on this fine Saturday morning.

She ran past Mullen's Ice Cream House. *A chocolate malt sounded delicious*. Maybe if she ate a healthy breakfast of fruit and cottage cheese, she wouldn't feel so bad about having a malt later in the afternoon.

Three miles later, she found herself running past David's house and wondering if she should stop. The spring formal was next week, and she had finally picked out her dress. It was a simple custard slip that went well with her silky blonde hair. David ended up going with a charcoal grey suit that matched nicely with her dress.

A sudden hot flash removed Jules from her fashionable thoughts, and she had to stop running. She was going to puke again. She didn't want to do it right here on Main Street where everyone could see her. She rounded the corner and found herself in the back alley behind Mullen's, by the dumpster. She puked again. Strange, this was the fourth day in a row that she had vomited. She'd been quite unhealthy with the drinking as of late, but she didn't think it was that heavy. Four days in a row was a record for her. She hadn't had her period in over a month either. She felt faint. She leaned up against the worn-out brick wall behind her and caught her breath.

"No, no, no," she said out loud and placed her right hand on her stomach. She pushed in and squeezed. Tears began to spill from her eyes. What if she was pregnant? What would she do? Her father would write her off as a tramp. God only knew what he would do to David.

Oh shit.

She walked the rest of the way home and thought about how she would tell David. By the time she got back to her neighborhood, she had decided that the smart thing to do would be to go down to Shuett's Pharmacy and pick up a few pregnancy tests.

2

Jules showered quickly and got dressed in comfortable sweats. She took her mother's car. At the pharmacy, she panned each aisle nonchalantly before searching for the pregnancy tests. She pretended to look at the surrounding items. It was a small town and she had to be careful that no one saw her. If word got back to anyone, including her parents, she would be the talk of the town. Lucky for her, there were only two elderly people in the store plus a clerk who looked like he might have been a drifter. She'd never seen him before. He looked to be in his late thirties and grungy with a beard and ratty clothes. Down the aisles of aspirin and other common medicines, Jules circled the store until she came back to aisle 3B. Again, she looked around the store and found that no one was there. She looked up at the security camera mounted to the ceiling in the far-right corner and wondered if maybe someone was watching her—someone that knew her father. For a moment, she conceived the notion that store security was calling her father while she stood in front of the pregnancy tests.

That was crazy.

The artwork on the pregnancy test boxes showed loving couples smiling at the blue plus-symbols. There were no pictures of depressed teens looking at the blue plus-symbols and there were definitely no pictures of ecstatic women holding a pink negative sign. Jules looked closely at the price tags on the tests and pulled the most expensive one off the shelf. She required quality on this purchase. Her parents taught her to save money at all costs, but this time she wanted to be certain, so she grabbed three of the most expensive tests. Just to be sure.

3

When Jules got home, her mother was standing in the kitchen looking out the small window above the sink. She liked to look out that window. There wasn't anything to look at but vast fields of grass and a forest in the far distance.

Maybe it soothed her.

Jules really didn't care right now. She had bigger problems.

"Hey sweetie, whatcha doing?" her mother asked.

"Nothing. I think I'm going to read for a bit," Jules answered, then realized that she was holding the pharmacy bag in her hand. Perspiration started to bead up on her forehead and she prayed that her mother wouldn't ask what was in the bag.

"What's in the bag?" Mary asked. Her eyes locked on the white paper bag with red print.

Jules' face turned beet-red, she could feel her cheeks burning, and her hands trembled with nervousness. "It's . . . ah . . . ." Mary settled against the counter and frowned.

This gesture meant that she had grown very curious and

the topic was now becoming an issue. Jules could sense that her mother was going to pry until she got an answer. A lie came to her, and she could feel the pressure, throbbing in her head, start to subside. "I have a yeast infection."

Immediately, Mary laughed and slapped her thigh. "I'm sorry, I didn't mean to pry."

Jules had never before felt so relieved. It didn't even bother her that she should feel embarrassed. She panicked a little when her mother took a step toward her, but she only hugged her and said, "Next time let me know. I have tons
of creams in my bathroom for that."

Gross.

"Okay. I was just a little embarrassed," Jules said.

"It's okay . . . trust me, it's not going to be the last time it happens either."

Jules smiled and headed down the hallway toward the bathroom. She had to pee. She'd been pounding down bottled water since returning from her run and on the way to the pharmacy, probably more than a gallon. When she sat on the toilet, a cold sensation swept over her, and she didn't think she could go. Her bladder was full and burning, but she still couldn't pee. She thought of David, of what he might think. Then, for the first time, she imagined that he would be okay with the pregnancy and would embrace it when she told him. They could work this out. If, in fact, she *was* pregnant. She didn't know yet. The warm urine coursed out of her urethra and for a brief moment she felt relaxed. Her bladder was settling. She held the small plastic application under her vagina and let the urine splash on it for a few seconds. It didn't bother her that she was getting the warm liquid all over her hand. She could wash her hands, but she couldn't wash away the pregnancy.

She pulled the small plastic stick from between her legs, shook it, and watched to see if the test was immediate. It took a few minutes, but then the color began to show. She closed her eyes and breathed deeply. She shook her head and shook the applicator again. Before her eyes was a light color that stood out bright in her mind. It was blue and it was positive. She wanted to break the damn test. There was nothing positive about this. Jules wanted to go to the University of Wisconsin Madison next year. Her first thought was that that would no longer happen. Anger and pain swam through her brain. Why had her first thought been about college? What about her parents? What about David? David's parents? Where would they get money to raise the baby? Would David shun her for becoming pregnant? Could she go through with an abortion? Her thoughts trailed back to the conversation that she'd had with Penny in the parking lot at school. Penny had said "it's different when it happens to you." And she was right.

But Jules was dead set against abortion. Her philosophy was that if it was growing inside of her then it was alive, no questions asked, and to terminate it would be to take a life. She couldn't bring herself to buy into the notion that it wasn't a human until after birth. But now, guilty as ever, she could see herself making an appointment at Planned Parenthood and having the pregnancy terminated. Tears welled up in her eyes and she thought that maybe the test was wrong. The box stated that it was not one hundred percent accurate. She quickly ripped through the second box and held it beneath her legs. She still had a little pee left in her bladder. This time it flowed well.

Again, the little blue plus-sign confirmed her fears. She went to her room and cried. She bawled into her pillow until it was soaked, then she sat up and it hit her: this wasn't a bad thing. *She was going to be a mommy.* A vision popped into her head: she was holding a newborn baby, and she was smiling, and suddenly Jules realized that her arms were configured as though she were already holding the baby. Her tears stopped and she leaned back and looked at the plain white ceiling of her room. A smile formed on her face. She was going to be a mommy.

Now she had to think about how she was going to tell David. She would tell him first, that way they could discuss how they should break the news to their parents. Jules knew that her dad would be furious. Her mother would be more sympathetic and probably happy in a secretive way. A bomb was going to go off, but in the end something beautiful would come out of it: a child. The spring formal was in a week, and she would tell David after the dance. They could go somewhere and make love, then she would tell him. Until then, she needed to get herself under control.

Jules made sure there was no paraphernalia left from the empty pregnancy test boxes. She collected the torn boxes and crushed them into her purse so that she could throw them out when she left the house later. With the sudden urge to hear David's voice, she picked up her cell phone and called him. He picked up on the first ring and Jules had never in her life wanted to hear the sound of anyone's voice more than she wanted to hear David's right now.

"Hey you, what's up?" he asked.

Jules closed her eyes and let a stray tear stream down her cheek. She was silent for a moment and then she smiled.

She was about to talk to the father of her unborn child for the first time.

"Nothing. I guess I just wanted to hear your voice."

"You're funny."

"I was thinking that maybe we could go watch a movie or something tonight."

"Yeah, I think that'd be fine. Can you pick me up? I don't have a car to use."

Jules wiped her wet eyes with the sleeve of her shirt and nodded her head as if David could somehow see her. "Yeah, I'll find out what time the movie starts and then I'll call you." "Sounds good ... talk to you soon."

Jules hit the end-call button on her cell phone, stood up, and went to her dresser. She looked at the small photographs of her friends wedged into the wood corners of her vanity mirror. She stared at Penny's picture and thought to herself that never in a million years did she ever think she'd be the one to have a baby while still in high school.

Chapter 9
With Fresh Eyes

1

Jules arrived at David's house around seven o'clock in her mother's black Jeep Cherokee. David hustled out of the garage door, stopped, and yelled something back through the door—probably to his parents. When his eyes met Jules, David smiled brightly and jumped into the Jeep.

They took off toward downtown.

The drive was silent for the most part, nothing of substance. It was hard for Jules to keep her secret. It danced, eagerly, on the tip of her tongue. She hadn't been to the doctor yet and her appointment with the OBGYN was next Tuesday morning.

Looking at David for the first time since she'd found out she was pregnant hit home. She looked at him with fresh eyes and he looked more like a man. He was a father. For now, he had no idea, but his life was going to change drastically. He would forever share a bond with Jules regardless of what direction their relationship went in.

After cruising Main Street for a while in silence, David finally turned to Jules and asked, "Why are you so quiet?"

"I guess I just don't have much to say right now."

David shrugged his shoulders and stuck a piece of gum in his mouth. Offered a piece to Jules and she took it. "Huh. You look like you have something to say."

Jules became flustered. Did he somehow know something? She'd never been good at keeping secrets. Jules shook her head. And with guilt washing over her, she lied. "I don't have anything to say."

The movie was short and neither of them enjoyed it too much. It was a run-of-the-mill slasher film where a group of young people went camping and ran into a pair of axe wielding psychopaths. The most exciting part of the movie was when David leaned over and kissed her. They made out for a few minutes, then stopped. They were getting too worked up. They needed to be someplace other than a movie theater, although they were the only ones there. The theater was small, and it was old. Most of the townsfolk went to Johnson Creek where the big cineplex showed all the latest films. The local theater, where they were now, only showed movies that'd already been out for a few weeks. But this theater was cheaper, which worked out well, for now.

After the movie, they walked to an ice cream stand and got a few cones. Jules had strawberry and David had

Rocky Road. A few other kids from school were out and Jules saw that the stoners from her math class had migrated to the back of the parking lot where she smelled the faint odor of marijuana. She imagined that ice cream was probably good when one was under the influence of marijuana. She'd only smoked pot a few times. Even then, she only partook in order for her company to remain comfortable and not think that she was a prude. She hadn't developed the taste for pot like most of the other kids. Penny liked to smoke it. But then, Penny liked to do anything so long as she wasn't *supposed* to do it. Just the idea of being naughty was enough to get Penny on board.

"Should we get out of here?" David asked while he wiped a few driblets of ice cream off his hands. "Or do you want me to go score some weed off those dregs over there?"

Jules shook her head and laughed. She couldn't smoke. She was probably over a month pregnant. "You know I don't like pot."

David looked at his watch, then stood from the picnic bench. "It's about time we got you home."

"I still have a half an hour or so. You want to go to The Garden?"

David's face contorted into a gentle frown. "And do what?"

"Talk . . . about life, love, and the pursuit of happiness. That and maybe fool around a little. Not too much, the clothes-on kind of stuff."

"I guess that would be alright."

Jules stood up from the bench, grabbed David's hand, and they walked back to the Jeep. "Do you know where you want to go to college next year?" Jules found herself asking.

David's head wobbled a bit with uncertainty. "I was thinking about UW Whitewater. I don't have the grades to get into Madison, like you."

"That's not too far."

"No, it's not. You think we'll make it?" David asked.

Jules felt a rush of cold shiver down the back of her neck. She didn't sense any real emotion or passion behind his question as it seemed forced. She didn't think that he feared losing her the same way that she feared losing him. But then again, it was just a simple question. "I think if we want to make it, we can. I think it's all up to us."

"I like that. It's weird, college being right around the corner and all. I mean I already know that I'll be going to school for business management and when I'm done, I'll work for my dad until he retires, and I take over the grocery store."

"Is that really what you want?"

"My head has never really been up in the clouds. I don't want to be a movie star, I don't want to move away, and I think what makes me happy is right here in Watertown. My parents are happy, and they have more than enough money to live the way they want to. If I stick to the plan, I can have all that too. I have no problem following in my dad's footsteps."

Jules pondered this with silent comfort. As the words left David's lips, they formed a vision in Jules' imagination. She could be his wife, maybe work at the store with him. Their parents would help raise the child while they both went to school. Neither Madison nor Whitewater was more than forty-five minutes away from home and they could see each other, and their child, on the weekends. For a brief moment, Jules knew that everything was going to be all right.

"That sounds good, David. It's a good plan."

"That's me. I like having a plan. Keeps me sane, you know?"

"I think I do know."

2

Five minutes later they were at The Garden and David felt a sick feeling in his stomach as Jules parked the Jeep in almost the exact spot that he'd screwed Penny. For a moment, David braced himself for confrontation. He thought that Jules must have found out. Jules never wanted to come out here. She knew why people came out here. She thought it was cheap, and she didn't like things like intimacy to be cheap. Now she was smiling at him, and his nerves began to ease up. She leaned in and kissed him.

"You seem a little jumpy," she said.

"No, I'm fine. You're just so pretty. I still get nervous around you," David said even though he was embarrassed by how artificial and corny he sounded.

"I'm so lucky to have you."

David kissed her. He dipped his tongue in and out of her mouth. His stomach was doing flips, but it felt good, and she rubbed her small hand over the top of his jeans. She traced the outline of his erection but didn't unzip his pants. In turn, David slid his hand between Jules' thighs and gently massaged them. He unbuttoned her jeans, fumbled his fingers into her pants and she swatted his hand.

"No under the clothes stuff. Wait until after the dance on Saturday, okay?"

David let out a deep breath and moved back into his seat. He turned to Jules and acknowledged how beautiful she was. He was lucky to have such an amazing girlfriend. He didn't deserve her. Another wave of guilt kicked him hard, and he felt a little nauseous.

He'd slept with her best friend.

What kind of jerk does that?

He wished that he'd never done it. He hadn't even really wanted to do it. Having sex with Penny was kind of exciting and it felt good, but the feelings that came afterward were horrible and he felt like an idiot for jeopardizing his relationship with Jules for a quick fling with a cheap slut. He imagined that Penny only wanted to have some sadistic leg up on Jules. Jules was smart, beautiful, and ambitious. She always did the right thing whereas Penny couldn't walk a straight path for more than a day without finding some sort of self-destructive act to indulge in, which showed everyone what kind of a person she really was: shallow.

David looked to his watch. "I don't want to get on your dad's bad side any more than I have to. I think you should take me home."

Jules put the Jeep in drive, and they left The Garden. Silently, David vowed never to cheat on Jules again.

Chapter 10
Confirmation

1

Arriving at the doctor's office, Jules was nervous, but not jumping out of her skin. She thought that she would be terrified. Waiting in the lobby was the worst part. She wanted this to be over with. There were two other people in the lobby, a man and a woman, no one that Jules recognized. A black and white poster framed neatly on the wall showed a mother and her infant child. They looked happy, and even though Jules assumed that the photo was staged, something about it seemed very genuine. The man waiting across the room from her looked to be about forty and the woman looked no older than thirty. The three of them sat, silent, while they waited their turn to be seen by the doctor.

Finally, a nurse came out of the back room and smiled at Jules. She said nothing, only shrugged her shoulder in the direction of the doctor's office. Jules stood from her padded seat and followed the nurse behind the cheap brown wooden door.

The office was small and the tests didn't take long. Jules was not surprised to find out that she was pregnant. In fact, she had already gotten used to the idea. The doctor was nice, fairly young, maybe thirty-five, and pretty. She had dark brown hair and brown eyes. She answered every question that Jules had and gave her a business card, explaining that she could call the office if she had any more questions. The last thing that Jules discussed with the doctor before leaving was about how to tell her parents. The doctor offered help if Jules requested it.

Jules left and drove to the ice cream stand on Main Street. She wanted strawberry ice cream. She craved the satisfaction of something sweet.

Jules sat at the same picnic bench that she and David sat on a few days ago. She had made up her mind to tell David about the pregnancy at the spring formal. Then they would *both* break it to her mother, and God forbid her father. For now, she wanted to spend a few days being a teenager. She wanted to go to the dance and have fun. She wanted to enjoy David and not have to worry about dealing with the current situation. She knew that it was a bad idea to drink alcohol, but if she only had a couple of drinks then it would be all right, and she wouldn't drink for the remainder of her term.

When she got home, her father was draining the oil from his truck. When he noticed Jules walking up the driveway, he pulled himself out from beneath the truck, wiped his hands on a dirty white towel, and walked toward her. There was oil smudged across his forehead and cheeks.

"Hey Jules, how was your day?" he asked.

Jules didn't want to lie to him. She'd been forced to lie so much lately. And she didn't like the way lying made her feel. But she had to, and so she did.

"It was fine. Do you need a hand with anything?"

"You can help by telling me where my daughter is," he joked while shaking his head, then he slipped back underneath his truck, whispering under his breath, "Can you help me with anything . . . ha!"

Jules entered the kitchen through the screen door that connected the house to the garage. In hindsight she realized that it was pretty odd that she would offer to help her dad with something like changing the oil. She was slightly spoiled, and she knew it. She walked to her bedroom without running into her mother, went to her closet and took down her custard-colored slip. She put it up to her body and modeled it in the mirror. She loved the way she looked in the dress, and she let the stress of being pregnant dissolve, for the time being.

Chapter 11
leaving home

1

It was Friday, May 1st. Jules stood in front of the mirror applying make-up. She hated putting on eyeshadow because she never got it right and it always ended up clumpy. Jules' mother hadn't allowed her to wear make-up until she was in high school. And even then, her mother wouldn't teach her how to apply it. Jules thought of her mother as a hypocrite, seeing as she wore make-up every day. Sure, her mother was modest about it, but she didn't know what it was like to be the only girl in school who didn't wear make-up. Jules noticed right away how many boys took interest in her once she started applying a little eyeshadow, cover-up and some lipstick to draw attention to her full lips. Penny had shown Jules the basics of applying the *stuff* to her face.

The first time that Penny had done Jules' make-up, Jules had stared into the mirror and thought she looked like a clown. The cover-up was smeared all over her face and the blue eyeshadow made her look silly. But when she and Penny got to the party, to Jules' surprise, all the boys were gawking. Even Mark, Penny's current boyfriend, had tried to lure her into one of the back bedrooms. That had been uncomfortable.

Now, Jules leaned into the mirror and conservatively applied the make-up. She dabbed the cover-up on first, then barely painted on a nice grayish tint of eye shadow to accentuate her hazel-blue eyes. Her hair had been done at the salon that her mother went to, down on Main Street. She barely applied the red lipstick, pressed her lips together and checked to make sure that she hadn't gotten any on her teeth.

It was five-thirty and David would arrive soon. They had dinner reservations with Penny and Mark at six-thirty, which would allow Jules' parents to snap a few photos before they took off. Jules turned the doorknob and exited the bedroom. She jumped, startled, when she almost ran into her mother. She must have been standing there for a while.

"Oh, you look so beautiful," Mary said while she clapped her hands together and then folded her arms in front of her chest. "Why do you have to grow up so fast?" Mary was shaking her head; her eyes were dampening.

"Mom, you're so corny."

"I don't care." Mary latched her arms around her daughter and Jules was afraid that she would smudge her make-up or crimp her hair the wrong way. Jules wanted to hug her mother back, but she had spent so much time getting ready that she didn't want to budge and possibly mess anything up.

The doorbell rang and Jules suddenly felt a quivering sensation in her stomach. She didn't want David to think she looked silly. She wanted him to love her and be turned on by her. *She was the mother of his child for God's sake*. And in that moment, before she answered the front door, Jules wondered if it was a boy or a girl growing inside of her.

David entered the house, completely disregarding Mary Benton, seemingly because he was too wrapped up in how beautiful Jules looked.

"Wow Jules, you look gorgeous . . . really amazing. Oh, I'm sorry Mrs. Benton, it's good to see you too."

Jules looked at her mother's adoring face. She looked like she wanted to cry. Normally, Jules thought she would have been annoyed, but now Jules thought that maybe one day she would feel the same way about her child as his or her date showed up.

"It's good to see you too, David. You look very handsome."

Jules felt the slightest bit of fear wash through her when the heavy sound of her father's footsteps came trudging down the hallway toward the living room. When he emerged at the mouth of the kitchen, he was wearing a welcoming smile and he winked at her.

"You look beautiful honey." He hugged her lightly as if he knew not to take the chance of messing her hair or make-up. "Look at our baby," Mary said to Richard.

"Don't embarrass me, mom," Jules pouted, half-jokingly. "I just want a few photos and then you can go."

They went to the front yard where Mary snapped about fifteen pictures of Jules and David. It went smoothly with very little pain and Jules kissed her mother and father goodbye.

2

Richard stood in the driveway and watched his daughter drive off. When David's car rounded the corner, Richard felt like jumping in his truck and stopping them. He didn't feel right about letting her go. If he were to stop Jules, make up an excuse to ground her, then she would hate him for a long time, but at least she would be safe, at home, with him. He fought hard and when he turned to Mary, she was crying also. They held each other as they walked back inside.

Chapter 12
Preparation

1

Ted stood over the six-foot-deep hole that he'd dug the night before. His excitement intensified while he thought about what might fill this small void in the earth later in the evening. He would go to the Jefferson House, and he would hunt again. Maybe he would find a score similar to the one he'd collected years ago.

He was dressed in his coveralls and a dirty white tee shirt. His Milwaukee Brewers cap rested neatly on the top of his head, casting a shadow over his eyes and nose. A smug grin formed across his face, and he went to the barn and sharpened his axe.

Afterwards, Ted went to his van and cleared out the junk he'd collected. There wasn't much, just a bag of lye and some gardening tools. He laid out a large sheet of clear garden plastic across the floor. That way, the blood from his next kill wouldn't make the van so messy. He'd spent too much time cleaning in the past when he'd used the Chevy truck. After a hunt, he'd had to clean the blood off the upholstery and windows. It was a tedious job and Ted didn't enjoy it. And with the van, it was easier to control the score. At least until Ted got home.

There was a metal cage installed in the back that made it nearly impossible to escape. The doors had to be unlocked from the outside. Ted had removed the door handles from the inside. Last night he had filled up the gas tank, and everything was prepared for the hunt.

Ted stood outside the barn now and inspected his land and his vehicle. Everything was a check. The sun had begun to set, and a breeze kicked up. It felt good on the back of his neck when it whistled by. An orange glow settled upon his property and the sky was calm and soothing.

After soaking in the view, Ted nodded. He was ready to go hunting. He would need to wait at home for a few more hours until he could move undetected through town, under the cover of darkness.

2

Ted sat in the living room and read an old "Hardy Boys" novel that he'd had since the 1950s. He rocked calmly in his chair and drank strong black coffee while his eyes scanned the yellow pages of the aging novel. At about nine-thirty, he got up and went to the kitchen, fried up five slices of bacon, and toasted a few pieces of white bread.

He ate his bacon sandwich. It was time to go.

Chapter 13
Dinner

1

David and Jules met Penny and Mark at the West Gate Inn restaurant, on the edge of Watertown. They had the best food in town. The white twinkle-lights strung along the front entrance gave off an air of elegance. The restaurant's dark wood made it cozy, and the dim atmosphere set a romantic tone. Most of the dates for the spring formal had made their reservations here.

It took David and Jules ten minutes to relax and settle in before they could look at the menu. They were busy making their rounds, saying hello to everyone, finding out where the parties were after the dance since the Jefferson House closed down at midnight. Eddy Wilson was having an after party, but Penny and Mark had already made plans to throw a party at Mark's house. His parents had gone up north and Mark had assured them that anyone who was drinking would stay the night. He, however, knew this wasn't the case. The house wasn't big enough to accommodate everyone that he had invited. The party would probably spill out into the garage where the keg was. He was sure that half the kids would drive home intoxicated, and he didn't care.

"I wish the dance wasn't out in the middle of nowhere at the stupid Jefferson House. I mean, that place is a crap hole," Mark said while he took his seat at the oval dinner table. He became annoyed when he saw that the tablecloth was stained. It looked like someone had spilled an entire bottle of ketchup on the tablecloth then simply tried to rub it off with a dishtowel. "I hate that."
"What?" Penny asked.

Mark pinched the tablecloth between his fingers and lifted it up for everyone at the table to see. "They know that the spring formal is tonight, so they dress the place down all shitty and up the prices on all the dinner entrees. This place is supposed to be, like, the nicest restaurant in town, yet they take advantage of the situation because they know they can get away with it."

"That's pretty interesting," Jules said, inspecting the tablecloth.

"No shit, it's interesting. If my parents came in here for dinner and the tablecloth looked like this . . ." Mark picked up his fork and examined it. Sure enough, there were large soap spots littered across the silver handle and the middle two prongs of the fork were slightly bent. ". . . they would stand up, show the manager how disgusting everything looked and then they would never eat here again."

"Who cares?" Penny blurted out while she dug through her purse and retracted a small bottle of chardonnay. She dumped her water out onto the green carpeted floor under her chair and filled the empty glass with the chardonnay.

Mark shook his head. "I care. The right thing to do would be to serve us with the same respect as their normal customers. I feel cheated and I can only imagine that the food is the stuff they should have thrown out last night."

David began laughing. "I didn't know that you cared so much about your dining experiences."

"I don't. I just don't like being duped. We're paying to be treated well, but the *establishment* here is taking advantage of the situation by overpricing our meals and lowering their service standards. We're being cheated." Mark leaned back in his chair. He hated the feeling that everyone thought he was too stupid to notice how wrong everything around him was. He'd felt this way his entire life. He was sure that Penny thought he was a moron too. Mark found himself wondering what Penny would say if he told her that he knew she had slept with David. He just didn't care. He didn't even know why he dated her. She was good in bed, but she slept with everyone in town, and it was embarrassing. After graduation, Mark had plans to leave this town and move on with his life. He didn't quite care how far away he moved, so long as it was far. Small town life just wasn't big enough for him. He would attend UW Madison in the fall, and he would study engineering. After that, the world would be his oyster. That was Mark's plan, anyway. Like everything else in life, Mark knew that his plan would have unexpected twists and turns, but if he kept the big picture in his sight, then he was sure that he'd be all right in life.

David asked Jules what she'd like to order, and Mark was surprised that she planned on eating so much food. He thought that David was surprised too, judging by how wide his eyes had grown when she ordered a side salad, the halibut dinner and an extra order of French fries.

"What . . . are you knocked up?" Mark belted out.

The frightened look that washed over Jules' face was enough to bring Mark's attention to a heightened state. Mark's intuition had told him enough, and he didn't want to offend or reveal Jules. He liked Jules. She carried an air of respect for herself that most girls did not possess. Penny was fun and that was all. What David had was more than a beautiful girl to hang on his arm. David had an intelligent and confident companion. Mark was sure that David would not be able to hold on to Jules for long. Girls like Jules moved on from places like Watertown. They had bright futures that beckoned them to move forward.

But what was this terrified look that she now possessed?

Mark looked at Penny and saw that she had noticed it too. Penny lowered her head and swigged back her chardonnay.

"God no," Jules said, panning the table for something to drink. Her fingers fumbled on a glass of water, and she drank it down. David's mouth opened and he looked as though he were about to say something. But the waitress came over, wearing a phony smile to go with her black bowtie and white button-down shirt. She must have been around forty years old and the crow's feet that mapped out from the corners of her eyes told the tale that she had probably drank for many of her years.

"I'll have the halibut platter, a side salad and an extra order of French fries," Jules said, then looked to Mark. "I'll run it off tomorrow."

"I'm sorry. I didn't mean to sound like a jerk," Mark said apologetically.

"Don't worry about it," Jules returned.

"I feel like I should say something," David threw in.

"Don't," Jules said with a smile.

The four of them ate their meals, calculated their bill, and divided it up into four parts. They left the restaurant and drove out to the Jefferson House.

Chapter 14
The Dance

1

Penny and Jules sat near the front of the Jefferson House, on a long picnic bench with blue and red balloons tied to the ends of the table. The Deejay played popular songs over the loudspeakers and everyone seemed to be having a good time. Jules was watching Mr. Smithy, the high school principal, while he stood at the hall entrance watching teenage boys hooting and hollering, raging about how much fun they were having. Smithy stood quiet with a stern look plastered to his face, scoping the area for any wrongdoing. Jules couldn't help staring at his balding head. It looked very abstract, as he must have attempted to dye the thin hair on top and the heavier hair on the sides with a brownish-red color. It made him look like a pedophile.

After a short while, Jules looked to the Deejay booth where she noticed David leaning over and shouting into the deejay's ear. Jules admired David's taste in music. It didn't matter if the song was classic, country, rap or poppy, David picked his songs by the story told within the lyrics. David had once jabbered on to Jules, for over an hour, about how much he hated rap music, but he enjoyed the late artist Tupac because his music had story, soul, and a message. It wasn't just mindless babble about *money, bitches, and cappin' muthafuka's*. Jules thought that maybe he could work in radio or some kind of music-related industry. He wasn't talented with a voice for singing, and he didn't play any instruments—that she knew of—but he was passionate about music in general. But he had no interest in pursuing it. He was very content with his future as a small business owner.

David left the deejay booth and made his way over to their table. He had a funny smirk on his face and when he got close, he grabbed Jules' hand and pulled her up from the table. "Dance with me?"

"I would be honored," Jules replied.

"Have you seen Mr. Wonderful?" Penny barked up at David, looking as if she didn't *really* care where Mark was. It seemed to Jules that Penny only wanted to gather David's attention so she could gawk at him the way she was doing now.

David blushed, and in that moment, Jules thought that she had been right about her paranoid ideas. Penny had a crush on him.

Had David maybe gone through with something?

Did he and Penny have something going on the side?

David and Jules made their way to the middle of the dance floor where another twenty couples crowded together. A slow song rang neatly from the speakers and set the mood. All of the girls rested their heads on the chests of their dates. Everyone on the dance floor shifted in slow circles while the sentimental song hit the sensitivities of the crowd.

"You look so beautiful tonight," David said, leaning back to look at her.

She saw the whites of his eyes go glossy and for a moment she thought that he would cry. She loved the way he was looking at her—adoring her—and it was melting her heart like butter in the hot sun. "So do you, David."

David shook his head and brought Jules in close. She could feel his bony chest against her breasts, and it was oddly comforting. In that moment, she finalized the decision that tonight would be the night. She wouldn't wait any longer to tell David that she was *expecting*. After the dance, she would take him to The Garden and they would make love, then she would tell him about the baby. In that moment, Jules knew that David would be okay with everything—with the pregnancy and her decision to keep the child. The way he had just looked at her was convincing enough to know that he really thought the world of her. She looked up at him and watched the corners of his eyes squint into thin lines as he smiled at her. His boyish face seemed to morph into that of a man. Jules thought she could see David older now, a fully matured adult. David would become more handsome with time too, once he filled out. It would probably take a few years, but he would grow into himself. Jules was glad when the slow song ended, and another began. She didn't want to let go of David yet.

Chapter 15
The hunt

1

Ted drove the white van down Briar Road. His eyes were watery, a symptom of his excitement. His hands were steady and strong on the wheel. Death and the destruction of flesh consumed his mind as he sped down the small country road that would soon fork onto the Jefferson House property.

The moon was full, the sky littered with bright stars that lit the night with a tantalizing luminescence. There hadn't been any clouds today. It was a clear, perfect, night for hunting.

Ted hoped that he would find a worthy score on this night. Every now and again he would endure the twisted knot of uncertainty in his stomach while out on the prowl, but not tonight. Tonight, he felt confident that a perfect score would cross his path and he would receive that which he sought after.

The small dirt entryway off Briar came up quick. The path that led behind the Jefferson House was barely visible, especially in the dark, but Ted knew where to go. He turned the steering wheel right and drove into the woods.

Ted turned the headlights off, making his vision hazy and he had to squint in order to see. Fortunately, the image of these woods was implanted in Ted's cerebral cortex, and memory was enough to direct Ted to where he needed to go. A small clearing opened up in the trees near the spot where he'd parked during his previous hunt on these grounds. He put the van in park and turned off the engine. There were a few rumbles and clicks, then the van went silent. The chirps and buzzes of bugs and insects rose in volume.

Ted got out of the van and closed the door silently. The heavy grass swayed across his legs and left warm dew on his denim overalls. He looked up at the moon and acknowledged that he was a dark creature of the night. He wanted to bathe in blood and feel the warmth of his score while its soul left its body.

Ted slithered through the bushes and trees to the forest line, about ten yards from the back of the parking lot, fifty yards from the back entrance of the reception hall. Just like back in 1980, he could hear the faint sound of popular music and the hooting and hollering of naïve and innocent teens as they celebrated their meaningless existence here on earth—on his hunting grounds.

Ted wouldn't go into the reception hall. Not this time. The last time hadn't been a school dance. It had been a wedding reception and Ted didn't stand out or look suspicious. If he were to go inside the Jefferson House and order a beer, the chaperones would wonder why an old man was hanging around a high school dance. Plus, the bar was probably closed tonight.

A shiver of excitement shot down Ted's spine when the first group of lovers exited the building and lit up cigarettes. The female was a brown-haired girl with bad teeth. Even at this distance, Ted could see the enormous gaps in her mouth. She wasn't beautiful. Her hips were wide, and her belly was flabby. Her date looked gangly. This couple was not the cream-of-the-crop and didn't meet the standard that Ted held. He only hunted the best—he wanted a healthy and able score. These two would be too easy. He wanted a blonde with some athleticism. The thrill of a challenge excited Ted. Usually, the boyfriend was just a bonus kill and was always a bit easier to kill too. Probably because Ted didn't give them the opportunity to escape: he killed them on the spot. He didn't like to play with the males. Ted enjoyed playing with the females because they were more fun to toy with. And there was more to do with them.

Ted lowered himself to the ground and crawled about fifteen feet to the left. From there he could feel the warmth of the cooling car engines in the parking lot. He lifted his elbows and pulled himself toward the space between the cars where he could clearly see the back entrance. The heavier couple went back inside, and it was silent for a long time. It must have been two hours before *she* came out.

A perfect score.

The girl came out of the entrance with a skinny boy. Her teeth sparkled and her hair was blonde and beautiful. Her dress was a yellowish color, and her legs were athletic and toned. The two of them stood on the cement walkway and kissed each other, long and hard. They didn't stumble and Ted quickly realized that they were not inebriated. Normally, Ted preferred his scores to be a little drunk, but if they weren't then "oh well." Ted skirted across a few feet of gravel to get a better look at them, but then another couple came out and joined them. The other boy was tall and muscular. He appeared much stronger than the boy with his score.

Ted's mind was set, this girl—the blonde—was his score. She was perfect and more than that, she looked strikingly similar to the blond he'd taken back in 1980.

Joan.

Ted couldn't wait to cut the blonde's head off and squeeze every beautiful drop of blood from her body. He wanted to cut her into pieces after he fucked her. His erection was so hard now that it sent sharp pains through his lower belly. Ted watched as the second couple went back inside. He heard the other girl yell something to Ted's score.

2

"We'll be out in an hour or so," Penny yelled to Jules as she reentered the Jefferson House.

Jules grabbed David's hand and dragged him through the parking lot. She wanted to tell him the news before her mood died. If she procrastinated any longer, she might not tell him at all. And she needed to get it off her chest. If she told him now, then they could both deal with the situation together.

What if it freaks him out? Their perfect night would be destroyed. "Let's go to The Garden. I want to go there," she said.

"Why? I thought we were . . . you know . . . slowing it down a notch."

Jules felt giddy and wanted to be with David. True, they had agreed to slow down, but Jules was in-the-moment, and she needed some kind of connection with him, something more than kisses and conversation. The night had been so nice and the way he had been looking at her melted her inhibitions. The loveliness that she felt had been the result of all the nice things that had happened throughout this perfect evening and now she needed to be alone with him. The Garden would be a perfect place to end the perfect night.

"Are you sure you want to do this?" he asked.

Jules was impressed with him for being respectful of her feelings. She kissed him—hard and passionate—on the mouth. Her lips were extra wet after the kiss. Their tongues danced playfully, and she felt liberated when she ran her hand over the top of his charcoal-colored slacks. "I have never been so sure in my life. I want to tell you something too."

"What do you want to tell me?" David asked, a quizzical frown forming across his forehead.

"I'll tell you when we get there," Jules replied.

David was digging anxiously through his pockets and pulled out his car keys. "I guess we're going out to The

Garden. What Jules wants . . . Jules gets."

Jules' lips stretched wide. David was on a roll and saying all the right things tonight. She hoped that he meant everything. "I like the sound of that."

3

Ted slithered closer and closer to the four-door Honda where the young couple seemed to be headed. The car was just out of sight from the back entrance of the Jefferson House.

Ted's nerves were steady and alert. The thought of lunging out at the couple was so fresh in his mind that, for a moment, he thought that he had already captured his score. The boy was leading the blonde toward the car. More importantly, he was leading her to him. The toe-ends of Ted's boots dug into the wet grass while he prepared to leap at the couple.

They were a few feet away from Ted and moving closer. Ted's right hand was cupped around his .44 Bulldog revolver and his index finger curled around the trigger. The safety was off. A few more steps and he would have them. His cold eyes quickly scanned the parking lot again. There was no one. It was perfect. They were only a couple feet away, now, and Ted was already pushing up on his knuckles in order to get a good jump on them.

A loud crashing noise broke the night's silence. The back entrance doors flew open. Ted stopped, looked up, and saw the other couple come barreling out of the reception hall. The blonde score stopped and turned back to the entrance when the other girl called to her, "Hey Jules! Mark and I are gonna leave too."

"Yeah, Penny and I might as well get my parent's house geared up for the party. This dance is lame anyway," the boy yelled out.

Ted was furious. He wanted to get the capture over with. He wasn't in his thirties anymore and it would be a challenge to capture two teenagers. Sure, he had his gun, but there were other things to consider. He needed total control over the couple or else they would be able to escape. He could control two as long as he killed the male score before they got to the van. Ted supposed it would be all right if he killed the male just after entering the van. For now, the plan was ruined. His sight was locked on this magnificent score. She was perfect. Her long blonde hair was neat and silky, just like the last score he had collected from this place all those years ago. He had to have her. But this other couple was coming toward the Honda. Ted wanted to kill. A thought crossed his mind. What if he stood fast, and at the opportune moment, shot all four of them? The thought was quickly dismissed. Shooting them wouldn't quench his thirst. Ted had a *ritual* and it had been *set* in his head. He wanted to play with his score and needed to get her back to his property. If he couldn't get the blonde back to his property, this night was all for nothing. And then his score entered the car nearest to him.

From Ted's angle, he could see the blonde's beautiful feet lift off from the gravel and slip inside the car. The door remained open. If he was swift enough, he could slither inside the car and take them.

Then he heard them talk.

4

"You're absolutely sure that you want to go out to The Garden?" David asked.

Jules thought that David had lost a bit of his excitement. "I really want to. Don't you want to go?"

"Yeah, there's nothing I want to do more than . . . that. I'm just thinking about last time."

"Don't worry about that. Plus, we'll be all alone and we can do whatever we want, and we can be as loud as we want," Jules said. Her hand slid down his leg and rubbed his thighs through his slacks.

Jules looked up at David and saw that he was licking his lips. She had excited him. She felt that at this point she had control of him. She closed the passenger side door and the engine rumbled to life. They left the parking lot. Jules leaned in close to the windshield when she saw something dart to the left of the car parked next to them.

Probably a rabbit or a squirrel.

As David and Jules left the Jefferson House, they saw a county sheriff parked at the mouth of the driveway. Jules was happy that she and David had decided not to drink until they got to the party. The last thing she wanted was to be pulled over for driving under the influence.

Jules looked in the side view mirror and thought, again, that she saw something moving away from the parking lot, something bigger than a rabbit.

5

Ted's anxiety diminished as he crawled into the tree line. His score was going out to The Garden. He knew where that was and he'd been out there many times, hunting small game—squirrels and rabbits. Other times he'd just gone out to reflect and enjoy nature. The Garden was a quiet and peaceful place. The local law officials rarely made it out there. Ted assumed that young people liked to go out there as a means for private fornication. He could go to The Garden and capture his score. If the couple went out there to have sex—like they had just talked about in the car—then he could intercept their actions and easily contain his score.

Ted ran through the forest as if he couldn't get to his van fast enough. He knew a private road that led to The Garden. He could drive down Briar Road over to Highway 26 and park next to the stream that emptied into the small man-made lake which sat in the middle of the reserve.

Ted hopped into his van, fumbled through his pockets for the key and switched the ignition on. The tires rolled to life, and he was on his way.

The blue Honda hit the highway at nearly the exact same time that Ted pulled up behind them in his van. There were no other cars on the road, which set Ted's mind at ease. Although he kept his distance, at no time did he fear losing them.

The young couple—the score—finally drove into the main entrance of The Garden. Ted continued on toward the rear entrance, driving for about a half mile up a small back road until he found the dirt service entrance that the Department of Natural Resources used. The DNR was the only law enforcement that Ted would have to worry about out here. But they didn't come out much at night.

Ted cut the van's headlights and used the moonlight as a means to travel down the winding dirt road. When he got to the lake, he pulled over and killed the engine. He got out and walked around to the back and opened the rear doors, found his work gloves neatly placed on the metal hook hanging from the left side of the van wall and slid them over his strong, callused, hands. He crept toward the water's edge.

The Honda was parked about twenty feet from the lake with the engine still running. Ted could see the outline of the two lovebirds as they got out of the car. He watched while the boy pulled the girl in and kissed her. His hands looked eager while they explored the blonde's body. He was squeezing her butt and fondling her breasts. Even though Ted was nearly fifty yards away, he could hear them panting lightly in the night air. The cool breeze carried even the softest sounds for a very long distance.

Staying inside the tree line, Ted inched his way toward the couple, careful not to step on any large branches that would snap or crack. He never overlooked the element of surprise.

Within a few minutes, Ted was thirty or forty feet from the Honda and his excitement was growing out of control. The situation had not played out the way he had planned, but it was still in motion. Until now, he hadn't thought about how badly this turn of events could foil his agenda. He didn't like surprises and never before in his lengthy career as a hunter had he escaped his principles. His score was in sight, and he should be pulling back, letting the score go, but he was too eager. He kept moving through the trees. There was something about this particular girl that he needed to have. Maybe it was because she looked so much like the last score he'd taken from the Jefferson House. Whatever it was, Ted was vacuumed in by her and couldn't turn away. For a moment, he stopped and shook his head, debating whether or not he should turn around, walk back to the van, and write this score off as a failure. It had never been a big deal before, to walk away when things didn't feel right. He stepped backward toward the van, then stopped—he couldn't leave, his impulses wouldn't let him.

He wanted this score; he needed this score.

Ted dropped to his belly and crawled across the wet grass, broken tree branches, and leaves scattered on the cold earth beneath him. With his .44 Bulldog in hand, he moved toward the young couple.

6

Jules' heart was beating fast in her chest. She loved the sensation of David touching her. His fingers danced across her body, exciting her. David was squeezing her butt cheeks and massaging her breasts. Her nipples were hard as pebbles and stuck out from beneath her dress.

David pinched them. She gasped and David parted from her.

"Are you okay?" he asked.

Jules melted when she saw concern wash over David's face. It made her want him more. "I'm fine, I'm better than fine. I'm great. Do you still have that blanket in your trunk?" "Yeah, do you want me to go get it?"

Jules nodded and David rounded the car and popped the trunk. He retrieved the blue quilted blanket, pulled the corners apart and flung it up in the air, spreading it out. At the edge of the water, he laid the blanket out for the two of them to sit on.

Jules walked over to David, removing her dress as she went. When he turned around, she smiled at him. His face had gone flush-red, and she thought that she could see his hands shaking.

"You look . . . amazing."

Jules unbuttoned his pants, and he lightly pulled her hair behind her head to stop the stray blonde strands from dangling into her mouth. It was liberating to be performing such a vulnerable act in the open, completely naked and exposed. She looked up at him. "I want you, right now."

David didn't hesitate. He dropped his pants and removed his shirt. Within seconds, he was naked except for his socks. Jules thought it a bit strange that he didn't remove his socks during sex, but it didn't bother her to the point that she needed to say anything about it.

Jules could feel her breasts flatten out when she laid down on her back. She looked up at the moon and admired how full it was. It felt magnetic. The stars were bright across the sky's dark canvas, which added a certain majestic element to the night's seduction.

David spread Jules' legs apart and he kneeled down and began kissing her. She watched him while he performed determinedly. He must have been very turned on and his tongue twisted strong and steady. She moaned loud with pleasure, and she let him up for air while her lungs pumped fresh oxygen through her chest.

"Wowwy, David. That was amazing." She kissed him hard and passionately, pushed him onto his back and crawled on top of him.

"I never knew I could feel this good," David said. He slid in, and she let out a yelp.

David rolled her onto her knees and had her from behind. Within a few minutes he pulled out of her and erupted onto her lower back. They settled, laid down on the blanket and held each other, remaining silent until Jules ran her index finger across his chest.

"I need to tell you something," she mouthed, barely able to contain her smile.

"What is it?"

Jules felt her nerves fray. Her stomach tightened. Telling David that she was pregnant danced on the tip of her tongue, but she couldn't say it. She froze up.

David sat up and looked at her. "Jules, you look pale. Are you alright?"

A hot-burning sensation welled up behind her eyes and in her throat and she cried, "I'm pregnant."

Jules could have sworn that David aged ten years in the two seconds that it took to tell him the news. His cheeks sunk in and his forehead spider-webbed with deep creases.

He looked away from her and began chewing on his lips. "You're sure . . . I mean, how do you know?"

"Well, I was sick for a few days—actually it's been longer than that now—but I got one of those tests . . . three actually, and they all said I was pregnant, so I went to Planned Parenthood and as it turns out . . . we're about six weeks along," Jules said softly. She sat up and leaned over onto her right arm. David wouldn't look at her. "How long have you known?"

"About a week." Still, he wouldn't look at her. She asked him, "Are you okay?"

He shrugged her off and said, "No, I'm not okay. That's kind of a lot to take in right now."

Jules ran her hand across David's face, and he swatted it away. His color was red and blotchy. He looked furious. His eyebrows furled and his mouth puckered tight. The lines on his forehead deepened further.

"We can't have it. When do we need to have the abortion by?" he asked as he stood up and began to pull his pants back on.

"I wanted to talk to you about that," she replied. She pulled her dress over her head, looked for her bra, but couldn't find it. "What if we don't have the abortion?"

"What . . . you want to give it up for adoption? Our parents will still know what happened. We'll go back to Planned Parenthood on Monday and we'll set up a time to get the abortion. That's it."

Jules felt rage run through her. She needed to fight David on this. He didn't understand what she wanted. He didn't seem to understand that she wouldn't have an abortion and that it was her body and her decision. And she was certain that he knew where she stood on the subject.

They leaned against the hood of the car, silent for a moment. David raised his finger and shook it in Jules' face. "You're not thinking about going through with this . . . are you?"

"Well yeah . . . yes, and I thought you would be more understanding," Jules said, pushing his finger away. She didn't like the way he flashed his finger in her face. It made her feel like she was his pet dog or something. It was degrading. "Plus, I personally don't believe that abortion is the right thing to do."

David laughed at her. "Don't give me that stupid shit . . . that's your dad's stupid shit. That's all you are . . . your dad with tits."

"It's not stupid shit, David. That's how I feel and I'm going to go through with this, whether you're with me or not! I'm not going to kill our baby. I wouldn't be able to live with myself."

David stepped close to Jules and his eyes looked black in the moonlight. They weren't sweet anymore and there was nothing compassionate in them. He leaned in until his mouth aligned with her nose. She was scared. She promised herself that she wouldn't back down from him. And then she was angry. She didn't like him invading her space like this. He was deliberately trying to intimidate her. He was trying to bully her into seeing things his way.

"Look, you fucking nim-wit, it's not a baby yet. It's not entirely our responsibility yet. We're nowhere near ready to have . . . *it*. I don't even love you!"

Those last words ripped Jules apart. She could feel the blade of emptiness slicing into the bottom of her stomach. Her throat swelled up and tears welled in her eyes again. Also, she felt the fight within her brewing. Now she was pissed. "You dead beat loser! There is a person growing inside me and whether you want to believe it or not, it is going to grow into a human being just like you and me. I won't take the life of someone who deserves the right to live. You can live in denial all you want . . . and if you want to take the easy road out . . . then I'll raise it . . . I mean him or her . . . by myself. I wouldn't want a loser like you raising my child anyway. I can't believe that I fell for someone like you in the first place! Take me home."

David was gritting his teeth and he looked madder than hell. Jules had hoped that he would see the light of what she had to say, but he obviously did not. He began walking in circles, clenching and unclenching his fists as if he were debating on whether or not to hit her. Then he quickly spun around and locked eyes with her. There appeared to be a deep sadness on his face. Jules lowered her guard for a moment.

Maybe he had come to his senses?

"If we had the baby . . . we would have to kiss off college.

Our parents would kill us . . . we would be throwing everything away. We can't have this baby; it will ruin our lives."

With her forearm, Jules wiped the tears from her eyes and took a step toward David. "That's not true. Trust me, that's exactly what I thought when I found out . . . but we can make this work. Our parents won't kill us. They'll be mad at first, but then they'll help us. We can still go to college and as far as the baby being a burden on us . . . well, it will be a lot of work . . . but we can still have a life and the baby will only enrich our lives." Jules was almost happy now. "You'll see when it's born."

A frown curved across David's face and suddenly he looked blank, as though he hadn't been listening to a word she said. He marched toward her and grabbed her arm—hard—and pulled her near. "Tell me again, when did you find out?"

"About a week ago. I just told you that . . . I didn't want to tell you until after the dance. I wanted us to have a good time tonight and not worry about it. I guess I got swept away . . . I mean we had such a good time and I got emotional . . . I just wanted to tell you. I thought that maybe you would understand and be okay with it."

"A week!" David screamed at her.

A twisting and sick feeling spread through Jules, beginning in her stomach and exploding up to her chest. David was punching her in the stomach. His fist smashed into the soft flesh of her abdomen just above her naval. She felt like vomiting, and she couldn't breathe.

More fight erupted from within her.

David was punching their child.

The life that was inside of her was being threatened and she needed to protect it at any cost. *Survival,* suddenly—and ferociously—illuminated her mind.

Jules grabbed David's arm and tried to force him away. To her success, she was able to twist away from his grasp. He wasn't very strong. He had more bone in his arms than muscle. She slammed her knee into his groin, and he dropped down.

Jules took a long stride and slid onto her knee when her ankle collapsed. She howled out in pain, then planted her hand in the dirt, forcing herself back onto her feet. She ran toward the tree line. Strangely, she thought she saw someone crouched down on the ground near the tall pine tree, close to the edge of the water.

Jules was just about to reach the forest's edge when she felt a blinding pain smash across the back of her head. Immediately, the throbbing knocks pounded through her head, and she was back on the ground with her belly in the mud. She felt helpless while she tried to roll over. She wanted to face David. Maybe if she were to look him in the face, then he would see that he couldn't do this to her. A terrifying thought swirled in her head and the cold truth hit her: David intended to kill her. He would take her life because of the baby inside of her. If she had only agreed to the abortion, none of this would be happening. They could be holding each other and looking up into the starry night sky. Instead, he was caving her head in with a broken log. She could smell the heavy scent of dirt and moss from the rotting wood as it slammed down—hard—against the back of her head.

The last thing that Jules saw before everything went black was the blood that trickled out of her nose and pooled in the dirt beneath her. The fight had left her. Her mind hadn't stopped fighting, but her body gave out, then there was nothing.

7

Ted was still in the bushes near a pine tree, crouched down low to the ground, fascinated by what he had witnessed. He'd come to The Garden to take his score but had ended up watching another hunter take *his score*. The twist of events was unsettling at first, but Ted had to admit that he enjoyed watching what had unraveled. In the war, he'd seen men taking the lives of other men, but never with dark desire. He enjoyed observing. He wanted to stand up and share the bond with this young man. He felt himself rising from the ground, but then stopped moving and settled. This kind of a hunt was meant for the hunter to experience alone. Ted would ruin the hunter's thrill if he were to announce his presence. Instead, Ted watched on while the young man stood over the lifeless score. He looked frozen with fear.

Ted remembered the first time that he had killed. He hadn't had time to stop, stare, and experience what he had done. His first kill had been in the heat of battle. The kill was a short Korean man with a silly green hat. Ted had shot the man from a short distance and watched blood explode— magnificently—from his chest. The man's thin eyes went wide before dropping vertically to the ground. After killing the Korean, the only thing that Ted felt was the icy wind while it chilled his skin. *Nothing more.* No remorse or guilt. The month was

January, and it had been freezing cold. Ted moved on and killed others that day.

Lying in the brush, now, Ted focused his aging eyes on the young man. The girl had called him David. And David was moving now, wiping his face with the sleeve of his nice white dress shirt, which was splattered with mud and blood. David fell backward to his butt and stared at the beautiful girl, the score that Ted had wanted to hunt. He supposed it was okay not to have this score. Strange as it was, Ted wasn't bothered that another hunter had taken what was his. The experience of watching the young hunter was enthralling. Ted wanted to walk over to the boy and sit with him. In front of Ted was a young hunter, much like himself; a killer. Ted had a bond with this boy, David, but he could not approach him. Instead, Ted got comfortable. He shifted his chest a few inches and settled in the wet grass. Then he watched the boy get up and pace. The boy looked to the entrance of the lake as if he'd seen or heard something. He walked over to the blue Honda that the couple had arrived in, brushed off his dress clothes and opened the car door. He raised his foot to get inside, then stopped. He turned and stared at the girl for a moment, then walked back to her, cupped his hands underneath her arms and dragged her into the bushes. He dropped her there like a bag of trash, got in his car, and left.

8

David drove through the darkness in a daze. He asked himself over and over again if he had really killed Jules. Quick flashes shot through his brain. Images of picking up the log from the ground after she had gotten away from him. Flashes of her blonde hair soaking up the blood that exploded from beneath her scalp, making her hair look black and slick in the moonlight. Then he saw her lying on the ground, motionless. He'd killed her. The reality of what he'd done brought tears to his eyes. Could he live with this? *No.* He would drive to the police station—right now—and confess everything. Yes, that is what he would do. It was the right thing to do. He slammed on the brakes and the car screeched to a halt, inches in front of a large poplar tree. David wished that he hadn't stopped. Crashing the car into the tree would have solved his problems.

He still could.

The thought of being dead brought a glimmer of hope to David's rattled mind. He stayed parked in front of the tree for a minute, just breathing. His heart rate slowed to a steady beat and his endorphins sent calmness through his trembling body.

No. He couldn't turn himself in. Yes. He could live with what he had done.

Living with this on his conscience would be hard, and it would be heavy, but right then—in that moment— David knew that he could live with what he had done. If he were to turn himself in, he would go to prison. Sure, he would be given lenience for turning himself in, but he would be throwing away his life. Not to mention that he would be throwing away the lives of his family. His parents would probably have to move away. If they didn't, they would be branded with shame for being the parents of a psychopathic son.

Is that what he was now? A psychopath?

Maybe he had been temporarily insane? David didn't know the difference between right and wrong at the time when he'd struck Jules with the log. He had blacked out. He was insane for the few moments that he had spent bludgeoning Jules. And he was innocent of the crime committed because he hadn't been in his right mind.

David put the car in drive and drove out of The Garden and onto the highway. There were no cars out and no headlights haunting him in the distance. He drove mechanically, following all road rules while he traveled home. He would have to park around the corner from his house when he got there, sneak through the backyard by the shed, take the shovel from the back wall, go back to The Garden and bury Jules. *Oh God.*

How could he have done this? The condom—if he had just remembered the condom.

They'd talked about having safe sex for weeks. They had planned the night that they were going to *do it* for the first time. David laughed out loud. The irony of this was funny for a moment. He felt like he was living inside of a sick and twisted after-school special. The sting of guilt stabbed him. One minute he was having sex with a pretty girl and the next he was performing the most heinous act of human nature; murder. The funny part was that if he had just worn the fucking rubber, she wouldn't have gotten pregnant. If she hadn't gotten pregnant, then they wouldn't have had the fight, and he wouldn't have lost his mind and smashed her head apart with a log. He laughed out loud again. This time he almost threw up because he found his thoughts humorous—and that was wrong. Laughing about what he'd done was depraved. A part of David that had been buried deep, deep, inside of him had enjoyed what he'd done. Pandora's box had been split wide open.

David parked his car on Third Street in back of a storage facility, ran a few hundred feet through his neighbor's backyards, and ended up near his mother's small garden where she grew a few stalks of corn, tomatoes, and green beans in the summertime. He slowly crept toward the back entrance of the garage and slid in through the white painted wood door.

The door creaked, and with each inch that it closed behind him, he imagined that his parents would awaken from the noise. They would come into the garage to see what all the clatter was, and they would find him taking the shovel down from the back wall. He had to take his chance. Jules' body was still out at The Garden, lying in a bush. If he didn't get there and bury her deep in the ground, then there would be evidence of what he'd done. There was no way that anyone could ever find out what had happened. He accepted that now. He had thrown around all of his options and this was the only one he could live with. He wanted to turn himself in. He wanted to do the right thing and move on, but it was more complicated than that. His life wouldn't be the only life ruined. His family name would be tarnished for life. He'd already destroyed the Benton's lives and they didn't even know it yet. The Benton's probably slept sound while David snuck around in his garage looking for a suitable device to bury their daughter.

He could do this.

David crept out through the garage door and quickly, yet swiftly, trotted back to his car with the large rusted brown shovel.

9

Ted stood up from the dirt and inched his way toward the score. *Not his score, David's score*. He could see the girl's foot protruding from the bushes where the boy, David, had tossed her. As Ted moved closer to the girl, he noticed that the thin fingers of her right hand were clawing at the ground. It must have been her nervous system expending its last movements. Nothing Ted hadn't seen before. But, as Ted moved closer to her, he realized that her fingers weren't twitching. She was trying to clench her fists. A rush of excitement struck Ted and he stood above her, looking down at her beautiful blonde hair and her stunning features. Even though she was beaten and broken, she was beautiful. He savored the image that she presented him with, then knelt down next to her and ran his hand through her blood-soaked hair. She still smelled of perfume.

10

Jules came back to consciousness when the heavy throbbing in her head pumped her body back into the world of the living. Aches and pains bounced throughout her body. The throbbing in her head was the worst. She wanted her father. She called out for him and found that she could only choke and gargle on her blood. She turned her head to the side and spit out a large mouthful of saliva and blood. It was thick and bubbly. Jules was still hurting—bad—but it was a relief to get the blood out of her mouth and throat. She could breathe again.

"Daddy," she whispered, hoping that somehow, someway, he would answer her. *A father's intuition?*

There was nothing.

When the silent compression of footsteps in the dirt sifted closer and closer to Jules' ears, she began to pray. She thanked God for the help that he had sent. It had to be her father. She almost believed it was her father, until an old man knelt down beside her. She didn't know who this man was. He looked too old to be her father and his eyes were hard, cold, and he was smiling in a way that frightened her. She rolled onto her side and tried to push up on her bruised elbow, but only fell backward. Jules' head was spinning, and she wanted to throw up.

"You okay little girl?" the man asked.

"Dad," she called out, looking past the old man.

"I'm not your dad. I'm not your taker either. I'm just the keeper that's going to take you to the next place," the old man said.

Jules felt confused. She didn't understand what this man was saying to her. He wrapped his hands around her throat and squeezed. She felt pressure behind her eyes and realized what this man was doing to her. He was finishing off what David had started. It was like a sick nightmare, and she wanted to wake up. She stared into his cold eyes while his hands choked off her airway and his thumbs drove wildly into the bone of her throat. A lucid sense of peace washed over her, then everything was silent.

11

Ted felt the girl's body go limp. She felt lighter in his grasp. He'd never paid much attention to this detail with his other scores, but her body had seemed to lose weight. He usually dismembered his scores while they were on their way out. He didn't choke the lives out of them. The lightness of her *being* boggled Ted for a moment and he let go of her. His first instinct was to *take her*. It was a ritual that he'd performed during and after each score. But then he remembered that this score wasn't his to take.

It was David's.

Ted rolled away from the girl until he was belly down in the dirt, lying next to her. He looked at her face. Even in death, she was beautiful. Why he hadn't wanted to take her was a mystery. David wouldn't know and would surely be caught for what he had done. Ted was sure of it.

David hadn't covered his tracks. He merely pulled his score into a bush where she would be discovered by the DNR on Monday morning.

Ted shook his head while he debated on whether or not to take this score home with him. It seemed like a good idea. Ted's fingers had touched the girl's warm, vibrant, skin. His fingerprints must be all over her neck. There were probably many other pieces of evidence that he had left too.

Ted stood up on wobbly legs and looked down at the beautiful creature before him.

12

David drove down Second Street toward Main Street where the road turned into the highway—the place where he needed to go and bury Jules. When he came to the stop light, he looked left. About a block down the street was the Watertown Police Station. The lights were on in the red brick building. There was no activity outside or around the station. The building appeared peaceful.

David signaled left and the stop-and-go lights turned green. He stayed put. There were no other cars on the street to pressure him into driving forward or turning left. He needed to decide what to do. Go left to the police department or go right and bury the girl that he thought he loved. The digital clock on the car stereo read two o'clock on the dot. He looked to the police station one more time, and realized it was now or never. His heart was beating fast, and his nerves were running rampant. He shakily moved his right foot over to the gas pedal and accelerated toward The Garden. He was crying again. This time he was crying because it occurred to him that he was a coward. He had committed a selfish and weak act and now he would have to live the rest of his days as a coward—the worst kind of coward.

The path leading toward the lake at The Garden was dark. David slowed down to five miles an hour. He was wide awake but struggling to see. His senses were distorted and his vision hazy from exhaustion. When he came to the clearing in the woods and saw the water glimmering in the moonlight, he turned off his headlights.

He was dreading the sight of Jules. Could he face what he had done? He didn't know. He parked the car as close to the bush as he could get and got out. Although he felt certain that no one else was there, he closed the door softly so as not make any noise. He walked to the back of the Honda and opened the trunk. He retrieved the shovel and walked over to the bush where he'd hidden Jules.

13

Ted's gaze shot toward the dirt path leading into the lake area when he saw a pair of flickering headlights fluttering through the trees. Panic struck him, and he knew this would be the end for him. He would certainly be caught if that was the DNR. Being caught was not an option. *He could handle the DNR.* In this neck of the woods, law enforcement was a joke and killing the official would most likely be an easy task. Most of the officers were overweight and unhealthy. Even in Milwaukee, the police were more equipped than what Watertown had to offer. Ted had to make his decision quickly—stay and kill or hide and watch. There was evidence here, and more importantly, a dead creature lying in the dirt. Then the headlights went dead, and all was dark except for the moonlight.

Ted crawled behind the thick patch of wild bushes to his right and inched beneath the brush for total coverage. His skin tore at the elbows when he pulled himself past a string of thorn bushes. A wave of relief washed over Ted when he recognized the four-door sedan—it was David.

The blue Honda came to a halt near the body.

Ted watched with heightened curiosity while the boy exited the car and walked around to the trunk. There was a click-pop and the boy removed something from the trunk—a shovel. Ted wanted to call out to the boy and educate him on what he was doing wrong. First off, he should not be burying the body here. He should take it elsewhere. Yes, it was a lot of work, but it was worth the price of getting away with what he'd done. Ted stopped criticizing and observed. He slowly nodded his head when he saw David grab his score by the arms and drag it into the woods. At least he wasn't burying it where it lay. The Koreans buried the dead where they laid at the Frozen Chosen Reservoir. But this score was probably David's first, and for that, Ted would allow him a bit of slack.

David was skinny and didn't look strong. He didn't drag the score along the ground with fluid ease. He was grunting and moaning. David went deep into the woods and Ted couldn't see him. He could only hear him dragging his score across the dry, leaf-ridden ground.

Ted slowly inched back out of the bush, careful not to make any noise, and crawled in the direction of the dragging sounds. Then, Ted found a large tree trunk and slithered behind it. The boy had set the girl down, and he was pacing around the small clearing. It was a good spot to bury her. The boy abruptly stopped and stomped back towards the lake. Ted stayed where he was. As curious as he was to see what would happen next, a familiar sensation was emerging within him. *Let the boy dig a hole and then make him your score.*

Ted's urge to take a score had not been fully satisfied and

his entire ritual hadn't taken place. *But why not take the boy?* The time and place were right, and he could get away with it. The whole experience of observing had been enlightening, but Ted's cycle had not been completed. He liked to take the female scores back to his property where he was able to perform his rituals.

Ted felt no desire to take the boy as his score. He wouldn't want to have intercourse with the boy: the thought was disgusting. He'd killed many men before, but there was no desire to *take them*. He usually took care of the males fast to get them out of the way. He could then take the female score without the headache of male resistance.

Ted watched as David came marching back toward the girl. He knelt down next to her and began to speak.

14

"I'm so sorry, Jules. I know you can't hear me, but I need to tell you this," David said, lowering himself to the ground. His knees were fumbling and shaky. His hands trembled and he had to hold them tight to his stomach. "I didn't intend on any of this. I wish I was strong enough to turn myself in. What I did and what I'm doing is wrong and I know it and I'm doing it anyway. I never believed in God or any of that, but I hope you're in a better place now. I don't know what came over me, Jules. I remember you telling me that you were pregnant and that you were going to have the baby. I'm not ready for that . . ." David was crying hard, and he was frustrated. He had to continue, even though what he was saying felt artificial. Honest, yet artificial. It felt like he was trying to tell her what she wanted to hear. She was dead, he'd killed her, yet he still couldn't be openly honest with her. Even in death, he felt that she was judging him. If he were completely honest, he would be challenging his beliefs. He shook his head, wiping the tears from his eyes. "I was a wretched piece of shit that couldn't go through with what you wanted to go through with . . . I can't handle being responsible. I'm too weak to raise a child. I'm too much of a pussy to tell my parents what we did and I'm too lazy to carry out the work that raising a child requires. I'm too selfish to even help you out with the pregnancy. I would rather fuck my life up all to hell than help you raise a baby that probably would have saved my life . . . I'm sorry."

David felt oddly relieved. A calmness loosened him up and his shoulders slumped. He was able to breathe freely again. He'd confessed, and for now that was enough to lead him into the dig.

The first shovelful was easy. The first couple of feet went fast. And David knew, from watching horror movies on television, that he needed the hole to be deeper. If he were to bury Jules in a shallow grave, the animals would get to her. They would dig her up and scatter her across the woods. He would be caught for sure. The hole needed to be deep so that he wouldn't get caught. If there was no body, then there was no crime.

David could do this.

After digging a few feet, David felt his back aching, bad, like the muscles between his neck and butt were being twisted and torn. His wrists were throbbing and probably swollen from the heavy workload. David wasn't athletic and he didn't exercise much. The most exercise he got was walking from the house to the car. His brand new white button-down shirt was soaked in sweat and his charcoal slacks were shredded and marinated in mud. He would have to burn his clothes. They were brand new, but his parents wouldn't inquire about them. What else would people ask about? What was he going to say happened to Jules? He was the last person to see her. Penny and Mark had seen them off.

David scooped up another shovelful of dirt and shook his head. Quick beads of sweat trickled from his forehead. He was exhausted. Water was on his mind—he was very thirsty. His lips were sore, and his saliva was dry and spongy. He'd done all this work without any water to hydrate with. An image popped into his head of the police showing up at The Garden—in the morning—and finding him laid out and unconscious from dehydration.

Good, maybe he would die from it.

David shook off the bad thoughts and continued to dig.

An hour later, the hole was dug. It must have been five feet deep. David was tired. He didn't think that he could dig any further. His back was rattled with knots that made him want to scream and his hands were blistered and bloody.

Great, one more thing he'd have to explain.

David leaped out of the hole, slipped on the loose dirt, and almost fell back into the opening. He clawed his way out. His strength was gone, and his body was on the verge of quitting. Once he was out of the hole, he rested on the cold ground. He looked at the face of his cell phone and saw that it was four-thirty in the morning. The sun would come up in a few hours and David would have to start thinking of what he was going to do and say. With that, a quick burst of energy—or adrenaline—shot through him.

David hopped up, went to Jules' body, and pulled her toward the edge of the hole. His breath quickened, but he had no time to be sentimental. He needed to bury her, and he needed to get home.

Looking away, David slid Jules' body into her grave. He moved feverishly to fill it with loose dirt. It went quickly, and David walked to the lake's edge and threw the shovel out into the water. The metal side shot up almost fifteen feet and arched into its descent. It hit the water with a splash and sunk fast.

What would happen next?

15

Ted watched the boy throw the shovel into the lake and wanted to smack him in the back of the head. Explain to him that if the body was found, law enforcement would probably drag the small lake looking for a murder weapon or anything related as evidence. *A shovel* would fall under that list.

The desire to take David as a score hadn't completely left Ted.

He watched David hobble to his car and again Ted thought to kill him. His fingers slipped around the grip of his revolver. *He retracted.*

It would be a liability to kill without desire. A content feeling washed over Ted while he watched David conduct his business. It was enlightening to watch the hunt from an observer's point of view, and he found himself enjoying the critiques that he'd come up with. There was a lesson that he'd learned here, and he felt educated further in his craft. Watching from the third person was a new experience altogether and he was glad that he'd been given the opportunity. Technically, Ted *had* taken the score. *It was Ted's Score.* He'd finished the job for David, but David had no clue. In that regard, Ted felt that he'd accomplished some of what he'd set out to do. Still, he didn't accept her as *his score*. He didn't even think that it could be called a *shared score*. The girl probably would have died from the blows she'd taken. David had brutalized the girl to the point that her brain had probably swelled and in a matter of hours she would have been dead.

The metallic cough of the Honda's engine echoed through the forest and Ted watched as David drove off.

Ted looked to the sky. It was still dark, and he felt tired. He walked through the forest toward his van and drove home.

Disappointment washed over him as his tires crackled over the cold gravel of his driveway. It had been an interesting night, but he was disappointed. He had planned on having a score to take home with him—to play with. He began to reminisce about the last score he'd taken from the Jefferson House.

Ted parked the van near the barn and got out. He wondered when he would have another chance to take a score. It might be a while. Still, he wasn't entirely unsatisfied with what had happened tonight, just disappointed.

Inside the house he removed his muddy boots and socks before entering the kitchen. He removed a thick slab of bacon slices from the refrigerator, found a frying pan, put bread in his toaster, and waited at the kitchen table with a glass of milk.

Ted ate his bacon sandwich and settled for bed. His dreams brought visions of his mother.

16

Ted's mother was wearing the gray dress that she wore on many days. It was long and draped along the hardwood floor when she walked. Ted was himself, only he was a small boy again and he was sitting at the kitchen table with a plate full of buttered toast. He was in a muddy set of overalls and his mother looked disappointed.

"You're not special. You're not strong. At best, you're one of those that are weak but tolerable and I don't even think that you've reached that status . . . The boy was weak—you saw him crying and weeping, yet you thought that he was like you. You felt a bond with him and then you let him go." His mother began to shake her head.

She slapped him across the mouth. He wanted to cry, but all he could do was sit. And suddenly, he realized he was frozen, paralyzed by the hold that his mother had over him. "I may be dead, but I'll forever live inside of you. You can't kick me. And until you can prove to me that you're strong again . . . I'll stay."

Then his mother walked over to the kitchen counter. It looked the same, only it rounded the entirety of the kitchen, surrounding all four walls. On the countertop rested the decapitated heads of every score he'd taken. They were smiling at Ted as if laughing at him.

The heads were neat and clean, no blood seeped from the stumps of their necks. Their skin was full of color, and they looked alive. Then they began to laugh at him. And when Ted looked to his mother for help—some kind of support—she turned around and put her hand to her mouth and joined the heads in a fit of laughter.

"You're weak!" their heads shrieked in unison, chanting over and over, "You're weak! You're weak!"

Ted could feel his cheeks burning with humiliation and he tried to remain cool, but he could not. He tried to stand, but he was restricted. Then the worst thing happened. His father entered the kitchen. The broomstick was still hanging from his rectum and the extension cord that he'd hung himself with was wrapped around his neck. There was a wheezing sound that escaped his lips, and he started laughing along with the heads lined across the counter.

Ted's father opened his mouth. "You're weak, like me," he said, looking to Ted's mother who was now holding a butcher's knife. They laughed hysterically while she plunged the knife repeatedly into his father's stomach, chest and neck. Blood sprayed across his mother, the floor and the counter.

Ted woke up in tears.

Chapter 16
Where is Jules?

1

Mary Benton woke up at six o'clock Saturday morning when she felt her empty stomach flipping and gurgling. There was a nauseating sensation that churned in the deepest depths of her belly. She lunged out of bed and stormed into the hallway, shuffled quickly down the hardwood floor, and pushed Jules' bedroom door open. "Jules, are you home sweetie?"

The bed was neatly made, and clearly hadn't been slept in. It didn't have the puffiness that a freshly made bed has. And right now, Jules should be sleeping in this bed. "Richard?" Mary called out to her husband. Her hands were shaking now, and she needed to see her daughter.

She scrambled to the cordless phone in the kitchen, punched in Jules' cell phone number and waited while it rang. On the sixth or seventh ring it went to voicemail and Mary left a message, "Jules, you didn't tell us that you were spending the night anywhere. Now you've got me worried . . ." She looked toward the hallway when she heard Richard's bare feet tromping along the hardwood floor. "If you get home quick, I can settle your father."

Richard was standing at the base of the kitchen, frowning. The lines on his forehead were creased deep and his hair was disheveled.

"She didn't come home last night?" Richard finally asked after a long silence.

Mary leaned over the countertop and put her head into her hands. "No, she didn't, and I'm really worried about her. I have a bad feeling. I just want to see her, so I don't get mad at her or scream. I don't want her to not come home because she thinks we're mad at her."

"Have I ever done that?" Richard barked at her. He walked into the kitchen, grabbed the phone off the wall and punched in the buttons. After a few seconds, Mary could hear her daughter's voice faintly echoing from the receiver, and for a moment she thought that Jules had picked up, but then the familiar sound of "leave a message" cut her hope off at the heart.

"Please get home as early as you can kiddo. Your mom is a little worried," Richard said softly into the phone.

Mary assumed that Richard was leaving the message in a gentle tone just to spite her.

"Was that necessary?" Mary asked. She was scared, nervous, worried, and frustrated all at once. She could tell that Richard was worried too. When Richard was lost in thought, the skin of his forehead scrunched down into a deep frown.

"Yes, Mary, I think it was necessary, warranted, and whatever else you think it wasn't! We told her to come home last night or call if she ended up staying somewhere. You spoil her to the point that she thinks she can get away with this kind of crap." He looked off at the wall—at nothing. He always looked away from her when he felt guilty about yelling at her. Mary hated it when he talked away from her. "I'm gonna call David Miller. Get his phone number."

"Do you really think that's a good idea?" Mary chimed in. She suddenly felt like the embarrassing mother-type.

Richard gritted his teeth.

Mary retrieved a phone book from the cabinet drawer and flipped to the back page where she had previously written down the cell phone numbers of Jules' friends. The fifth phone number on the list was David's. She turned the phone book around clockwise so that Richard could read her scribbled numbers, then slid it toward him on the smooth countertop. He punched in the phone number and waited for it to ring.

2

David sat in his leather computer chair in his bedroom. It was morning, and although he was tired to the point of delirium, he could not sleep. Thoughts of what he'd done to Jules swirled guiltily in his head, stabbing at his brain. Just yesterday he had been walking hand-in-hand with her at school before the end of fifth period chemistry. They were talking about going to the dance and attending the party at Mark's house afterward. Life had been simple yesterday, and today it was something completely different. David's entire being had changed drastically within the few minutes that it had taken him to end Jules' life. The honest voice in the back of his head relayed to him that he was a selfish murderer with no sense of responsibility. He looked around his room at the walls where pictures of Aaron Rodgers, quarterback for the Green Bay Packers, a movie poster of *Jaws*, and a few random framed pictures hung in neat rows. One of the framed photos was of David and his father in a boat on Lake Michigan during a fishing trip. They had fun that day. It was one of the more sentimental days he'd shared with his father. They had talked about life and at one point while David reeled in his fishing line, his father had told him something that really stuck. He'd said, "Life is always going to come down on you . . . and hard. The only thing you can do is to keep on living and then live some more." David didn't really understand what his father had meant at the time, but right now he imagined he was gaining an understanding. *He needed to go on, no matter what.* His parents needed him, and they needed him to be successful. If he could get back on track, change, then he might be able to salvage the rest of his life. That's what he would have to do. The phone rang on his desk.

The caller ID read "Jules Home" and David picked up the phone and held it in his hand. For a split second he wondered if all of this could be a dream. That maybe it was a bad nightmare. Was Jules calling him?

It had to be Jules' father.

David's thumb traced the edge of his flip-top phone receiver where he would either flip it open and answer the call, or simply hold it shut and let it go to voicemail. After taking a deep breath, he answered, and was surprised that he could sound cheerful while he lied. "Hey Jules, what's up? It's kind of early isn't it?"

There was only silence on the other end and David wondered if his deceit had been effective. Also, he was somewhat impressed by how quickly he'd been able to come up with this lie. It was quick and confident.

"This is Richard Benton, David."

"Oh, hey Mr. Benton, how are you?" David said with a smile. Although no one was watching him, he wanted to look the part. He thought of himself as an actor in a movie.

"I'd feel a lot better if I knew where my daughter was, David. The last time we saw her was with you."

A guilty pain pinched at David's stomach, but he didn't drop his guard. If he were to continue living his life, he would need to get through this. "I dropped her off last night and went home . . . it was a little before one, I believe. Do you want me to call her cell phone?"

"I already tried that."

"Maybe she's out for a run?" David asked with a false hint of curiosity in his voice.

Richard's voice was low and monotone. "Her running shoes are in her room. She never goes running this early anyway. And besides, she didn't wake us up when she got home last night. She always wakes us up."

"We went to the dance out at the Jefferson House last night and left at about midnight. We were going to go to Mark Tisdale's house afterward, but we went to Lincoln Park instead and talked for a while . . . and then I dropped her off at home. We sat in the driveway for a few minutes talking."

There was another long silence and Richard's voice became raspy. "Will you try and find her, David? It would mean a lot to us."

"Of course, she's probably just running an errand or something. I'm sure it's nothing to worry about," David said. There was a wad of phlegm stuck in his throat that he wanted to cough up, but he decided to wait until the conversation with Jules' father was over. He didn't want to cough because it might make him sound nervous, and he was doing too good of a job lying to mess up his momentum with a nervous cough. Certainly, David was being paranoid, but he had good reason to be paranoid—he'd murdered the daughter of the man he was talking with on the phone. David was trying to tell Mr. Benton that he should calm down, when in fact his entire world should be falling to pieces.

"I hope so, David," Richard said, then the dial tone swarmed across the connection. David had an intuition that Richard Benton wasn't buying his story. There was something challenging in his voice. David stood up and walked over to his closet. On the floor, in the back, below the tee-shirts neatly hung on wire hangers, was a small duffel bag containing the dress clothes he'd worn to the dance. They were stuffed tightly into the small green nylon bag.

He would burn them. There was a quarry out on Route 7—he could burn the clothes there, scatter the ashes, be rid of the evidence—at least the evidence that he knew of.

3

Richard set the cordless phone back on the charger and turned to Mary. She looked sick. Her color was fading, and her skin was ashen. Perspiration gleamed lightly on her forehead. She rubbed her stomach and frowned, shaking her head. "I think I'm going to be sick." She darted toward the hallway. Richard could hear the bathroom door fly open and the heaving sound of his wife hurling into the toilet bowl, and he wondered what she had in her stomach that she could be throwing up. The last time she'd eaten was at about seven-thirty last night. Her stomach should be empty.

A sinking sensation expanded in the pit of Richard's stomach. He couldn't help but think that David was lying about something. He didn't sound nervous at all, and his tone was that of genuine concern.

Was David that devious?

The toilet flushed and Mary came back into the kitchen. Some of the color had returned to her face and her cheeks were flushed pink. Her lips were chapped-red and there was a tiny string of saliva dancing off her chin.

"I need to do something, Richard. I can't just stand around and think the awful things that I'm thinking."

Richard wanted to slap his wife for implying that something horrible had happened to their daughter. Jules was probably fine. Maybe she was running. She had gotten new running shoes in the past without telling them, which would explain why her old running shoes were still neatly staged in her closet. Still, his wife's anxiety was warranted, and it was real. A horrid feeling was developing within him, and he couldn't ignore it. "We'll wait another hour, then we'll call the police. In the meantime, we'll call everyone that Jules knows."

For the next hour, Richard and Mary called every one of Jules' friends that they had a listing for. They called Penny Sloan, and they called her boyfriend Mark. The few friends they talked to all said the same thing—that Jules and David looked happy, and everyone had seen them at the Jefferson House having a great time. They had left together around midnight.

With each call, Richard grew more and more certain that David had something to do with Jules being missing. The only other option that crossed Richard's mind was that someone had kidnapped Jules as David dropped her off. And that was a very hard theory for him to believe.

"It's been an hour," Mary said, holding out the phone for him. He punched in 911 and waited for the dispatcher. The dispatcher's monotone words hit him harder than he imagined they would, and he was unable to speak. The woman sounded robotic.

"911, what's your emergency?" The soft female voice asked with calm urgency.

It took Richard almost thirty seconds to answer. The dispatcher had to ask again, "What's your emergency?" before he finally answered.

Richard met Mary's eyes as his mouth opened into the receiver. "I need to report a missing person."

"Let me direct you to a detective," the dispatcher returned without losing her mechanically urgent tone of voice.

Richard wondered which detective he would end up dealing with. There were only a few on the force, maybe eight at the most. It was a small town and most of the detective work was delegated to finding teen vandals and investigating minor thefts, or so he assumed. Richard had gone to school and grown up with most of the older policeman on the force and a good percentage of them were fairly bright people. A few of the officers had control issues, which came with the job. But Richard only knew of one bad cop. Officer Drew Kay—he was as dirty as a small-town cop could be.

"This is Detective Finley, how can I assist you?" the voice on the other end of the phone asked. His voice was deep and raspy with a sympathetic tone.

"My . . . I need to report my daughter missing," Richard said. And as the words left his lips, he felt his heart hammer down to his stomach. His face filled with blood and his cheeks burned. It was as if the words escaping Richard's mouth drove his dread thoughts into reality.

"When was the last time she was seen?" Detective Finley asked.

"Last night. She was with her boyfriend at the spring formal . . . the Jefferson House . . . they were seen leaving together," Richard said while he walked into the kitchen and took a seat at the table.

"How old is your daughter?"

"Seventeen."

"She ever stay out this late before?"

"Not without calling. Her boyfriend claims that he dropped her off around one o'clock in the morning. She never woke us up and she's gone now. I don't think she ever made it home."

"What's your daughter's name?"

"Jules Benton. I'm Richard Benton, her father."

"Okay, Richard. Usually someone needs to be missing for forty-eight hours or more before we can make it official. I'll stop by in a half an hour and we'll talk. That sound good?"

"Yes, my wife and I would appreciate that," Richard replied, and Finley hung up.

Richard set the phone on the table and turned to Mary. "A detective will be over in a half an hour."

Richard watched his wife slowly nod her head. "You want coffee?"

"Yes, please."

Richard and Mary sat quietly in the living room sipping their coffee while they waited for Detective Finley to arrive. Finally, he pulled up in the driveway about forty-five minutes after the phone conversation. Richard could sense that Mary was a bit frustrated with the detective's tardiness. Standing up from the reclining chair, Richard went to the front door. He peered out at Detective Finley with curious eyes. He knew many of the men on the police force, but he didn't know this man. He was large, probably six foot three inches or so and he was bulky, not fat. He looked like an offensive lineman and was dressed in wrinkled black slacks and a white button-down shirt with a blue tie that brought out his blue eyes. His face was puffy but handsome.

Richard extended his hand out to the detective. They shook and Richard moved aside so that Finley could enter. "This is my wife, Mary."

Richard watched as Detective Finley took in the sight of Mary. This wasn't the first time that someone had been struck by Mary's beauty. Even in her current condition, she was stunning for her age. Finley walked over to her and extended his hand. She took it and motioned for him to sit down on the couch.

Finley pulled his black slacks up near the hips and sat down. His blue tie was loosened and looked odd against his white button-down shirt. The detective's hair was silver and groomed neatly. Richard guessed that the detective was about fifty.

"Are you a native of Watertown?" Richard found himself asking with a note of curiosity.

"No. I'm from out of state. My wife is from Fort Atkinson. We met in California and just moved here about six months ago. I get asked that a lot though. Small towns . . . everyone really does know everybody around here. It's kind of nice. Different . . . but nice," Finley answered with a friendly smile. "Now, your daughter, Jules, she ever stay out all night and not come home before?"

It was the same question that Finley had asked on the phone earlier, and Richard found himself wondering if this was some kind of detective work. Maybe Finley was testing him, to see if his answer would change. "No. Like I said on the phone earlier, this is the first time Jules has pulled this. And her boyfriend, David Miller, claims that he dropped her off . . . here."

"You happen to have David Miller's phone number and address?" the detective asked.

"Sure do," Richard responded and handed him a small piece of notepad paper. He'd already written down David's phone number and address for the detective.

"Have you already called her friends? Anyone who might know her whereabouts? And is there anywhere else you think she may have gone?"

"We called her friends." Richard looked at his wife while he answered. "We've called everyone we know, and they all say the same thing . . . that Jules and David left the Jefferson House around midnight. They were supposed to be going to a party at Mark Tisdale's house, but they never showed up."

"Uh, huh." Finley reached into his pocket and pulled out a small notepad. He peeled back a few pages, retrieved a black and white Bic pen from his shirt pocket, shook it, wrote something down. "Look, I know you're worried, but usually these things turn out just fine. Most of the time, the kid in question is hung over and doesn't want mom and dad to know that he or she got drunk the night before. The boyfriend might be covering for Jules to keep her out of trouble. Teens think like that. I'm going to start looking into this right away." Finley smiled at Mary. Richard felt a hint of jealousy sting at him. He didn't know why, but he didn't like the way Detective Finley was looking at his wife.

"Now," Finley held his hands up as if he were stopping traffic. "Just on the off chance . . . and I have to ask . . . is there anybody that Jules has had a conflict with lately? Any enemies?"

Richard turned to Mary, bewildered and frowning. In unison, they shook their heads. Then Richard threw a sly smirk in the direction of Finley. "I'm not real big on David, her boyfriend. I don't trust him."

Mary crossed her arms and shot him a dirty scowl. "What does that have to do with anything?" she barked.

Richard's defenses suddenly went into overtime, and he leaned in toward his wife, locking eyes with her. "I don't like him, never have. He said that he dropped her off—here—last night, and to tell you the truth I think he was lying through his teeth. We can't find our daughter and I'm worried. And yes, I would like for the record to indicate that I think there is something off about David."

Finley's eyes widened when Richard raised his voice. He seemed to be listening closely to everything Richard was saying. He jotted something down in his notepad, closed the cover and stood from the couch. "Look, for what it's worth, the last thing that's going to help this situation is tearing at each other's throats. I'm sure this will all amount to nothing but miscommunication, in the end. So, let's all just take a deep breath and be civil. Okay?"

Richard felt guilt pierce through his conscience. He nodded his head. "You're right, I'm sorry hon."

Mary nodded back, hopefully accepting Richard's apology as she usually did. Richard walked Detective Finley to the door and watched him walk to his car and drive away.

The next few hours were nail-biting, and it took all of Richard's energy not to take his stress out on Mary. To stay busy, they called all of Jules' friends again asking if they had heard from her.

The phone finally rang about three hours after Finley left. Time froze for the moment. Richard and Mary both shot their eyes toward one another, then toward the phone, paralyzed with anticipation. After the second ring, they both darted toward the kitchen. Richard answered the phone. "Jules?"

"No, it's Penny Sloan. I was just wondering if you guys had heard from Jules yet?"

"No Penny, we haven't. Thank you for calling though, we appreciate it," Richard replied, genuinely grateful to Penny for her concern.

"Is there anything I can do to help?" Penny asked.

"Just keep calling around and if you hear anything, please, please, give us a call."

"That I can do."

Richard set the phone down and turned to Mary. It wrenched his guts to see the sorrow in her face. She wrapped her arms around him tightly. "We can get through this, right? Together we can get through this?"

Richard parted from Mary and met her eyes. He didn't think he could remember a time that he'd seen her eyes so red in all of his life. His gaze became focused on the small yellow flecks that surrounded the blueness of her eyes. He hadn't paid this much attention to the details of her eyes since they were much younger and much more passionate about each other. Mary was the love of Richard's life and with time their love had evolved into something much deeper and more intimate than the details of each other's eyes. Their love wasn't as intense and physical as it had once been and the need to constantly be within each other's presence wasn't as overbearing. The unity of their marriage had strengthened to its highest level and now it was being tested.

"We don't know that anything bad has happened to her. She could be out running. She could be sleeping off a bad hangover," Richard said. He would have continued, but the slow and helpless fashion with which Mary now shook her head silenced him.

"If she were okay, I wouldn't feel this void in my heart," Mary said. She turned away and walked down the hallway, dragging her bare feet across the hardwood floor. Richard stayed and watched the phone, anxiously waiting for it to ring again.

Chapter 17
The Past Reawakened

1

Robert Grabske waddled down the cracked sidewalk on the way to his favorite diner at the corner of First and Main. His joints, especially his hips, cried painfully with each step that he took. He'd parked his car behind Watertown Mutual, the town's most successful independent financial institution. The small parking lot at Charlie's Diner was always full and—despite the pain in his legs—he needed the exercise. There were only seven spots to park in at the diner and they went fast. Parking at the bank gave Robert the opportunity to walk a few blocks and catch some fresh air. The blood flow in his legs wasn't what it used to be, and even if he only walked a short distance, he felt as though he'd fought the good fight, if only for a day.

Robert stopped a few feet in front of the diner and looked down Main Street. There weren't many cars cruising down the two lane drag, which wasn't unusual given that not much happened on Monday mornings in Watertown. Robert hunched over a rusted-out newspaper stand, placing two shiny quarters into its slot. He remembered the days when a newspaper only cost a nickel; you could walk by the Watertown Daily Times office, throw your coins into a small cardboard box and grab your paper. It was the honor system, a thing of the past in these modern times, much like his youth. The date on the newspaper was May 3rd and the headline read "Teenage Girl Missing."

Robert brought the paper up close to his face; he'd left his reading glasses in the car. Sometimes he brought them along, and other times he did not. Usually, he was too caught up talking with his fellow "old-timers" to care about reading his paper. The old codgers had better things to talk about, like the good old days, back pain, and how they wished their wives were still alive because they missed all the nagging. Of course, they didn't mean it to be disrespectful—quite the opposite. The cheery old men missed their companions dearly and felt like they were simply drifting along through the final stages of their lives until they could leave this world and join their loved ones. Robert had lost his wife Gina three years ago to lung cancer. She had been coughing for a few weeks, finally went to the doctor, and within six weeks she had passed. They had had time to say their goodbyes and now Robert was very lonely. He knew that *his time* would come soon, and he wasn't afraid of dying. He'd lived a good life, raised a few children—two boys—both of whom had gone off to California and started their own lives. Neither of them had children and they rarely came home to visit.

Robert had raised his family, watched his children grow into adults and move on with their own lives. These days, it seemed like the only thing left to do was die. And he had some good friends to share his journey to the end with. In fact, he was meeting his oldest and dearest friend, Tim Fuller, with whom he had served thirty-five years on the Watertown Police Force with.

Tim had moved up the ranks much faster than Robert, but he was okay with that because his passion had been his family and Gina always came first. Being a policeman was Robert's way of serving his country and community and he was proud of what he did for a living. It was small town living with small town crime. The worst he'd ever dealt with was a missing person case in 1980. A young couple had gone missing from the Jefferson House. Robert had a good suspicion that the couple was dead, but the family had never given up hope.

As Robert stared down at the day's newspaper, he was brought back to that crime. The girl on the front cover looked very much like Joan Neverman, the teenage girl that had gone missing along with her boyfriend. It was a peculiar thing that Robert was able to remember her name and not the boy's. He'd forgotten so many things in his old age, but the disappearance of those young kids had stayed with him for a long time; decades. He'd wished that the disappearance had never occurred, even though it was a *real* crime and Robert's only *real* investigation during the course of his career in law enforcement. He was the lead detective on the case and although he didn't get very far, he had his suspicions. His recollection of the case was flashing back at him like a strobe. The case hadn't been investigated for any length of time. The FBI had ended up stepping in after a few weeks with their fancy resources and spent a lot of time and money coming up with nothing.

Robert jumped and spun around, startled, when he heard the sound of fists pounding on the diner window behind him. He thought he'd pulled a muscle in his neck and brought his free hand up to massage it. There, staring through the glass was a wrinkled face with spotty pink skin and thin white hair. Robert smiled when he recognized the man as his friend, Tim Fuller. Through the window he could hear Tim say, "Come inside, old-timer!"

Robert folded the newspaper in half, tucked it under his arm and walked inside. Like always, he struggled to lift his shaky legs up over the abnormally high cement steps that led upward into the dining room. He waved to Norma and Jenny, the two young waitresses who were also students up at the Christian College near the west end of town. They were nice girls with good attitudes that came by and sat at the tables with their customers. They didn't just fill the coffee cups and deliver food; they provided a little companionship.

After Robert said hello to the girls, he walked toward the back booth and took his seat with Tim.

"I already ordered you a cup of coffee, but don't expect me to pay for it. I collect the same pension you do, so don't try and pull one over on me," Tim said. A scowl formed on his face, making him look constipated.

Robert shook his head. "Every morning you blab about the same thing and try to skip out on the bill when it comes around. Yes, we collect the same pension, but you never let that stop you from letting me pay your bill half the time we meet here."

Tim nodded his head and smiled. "You really are a good friend then. So, there any good lies in that newspaper you just wasted fifty cents on?"

"I'm sure there are. I haven't gotten around to reading any of them yet. I like to let you bore me before I start reading my paper."

The wrinkles creased deep across Tim's face. "Always the gentleman."

Robert placed his newspaper near the metal menu holder and turned his attention back to Tim. It was hard for him to turn away from the smiling photo of the young girl on the front page. The similarity between Joan Neverman and this missing girl was so striking that it troubled his fine morning. Unable to control his urge, Robert unfolded the newspaper and spread it out across the table for Tim to see.

"What the hell are you doing?" Tim asked.

"You remember that couple that went missing back in eighty?" Robert asked.

"Yes, you senile old bastard, I remember the couple that went missing."

Robert pointed to the picture of the missing girl. He read a few lines down to where it stated that her name was Jules Benton. "Doesn't she look like the girl . . ."

Tim's scowl was gone and now he looked angered. Robert had worked with Tim long enough to know he wasn't amused. "What does that have to do with anything?" Tim asked.

"Well, for one thing, she went missing after a dance at the Jefferson House and second, she looks just like the girl that went missing back in eighty. It's the same face at the same location," Robert said, suggesting that Tim should see the relevance. "I think that there might be a relation here, other than the obvious. I've read that those serial killers have a particular flavor they like to stick to . . . a specific look."

"And what the hell are you gonna do?" Tim grunted. He panned the restaurant to make sure no one was listening in on their conversation. Not that anyone would have any interest in what a couple of eighty-year-old-men were blabbing about.

"Something . . . I feel like I should do something," Robert replied.

"That case has been closed and done with for twenty some years. Don't go picking at scabs that aren't meant to be opened. And the reason they shouldn't be opened is because you have no reason to. Nothing you've said here this morning makes any sense except that the last place that girl was seen was at the Jefferson House and that she has blonde hair."

Robert quickly realized that Tim had already read the newspaper. Tim was hard to convince—he was smart—

and he was thinking the same thing that Robert was; that there was a connection. "I know you're thinking the same thing I'm thinking, and I think that we ought to tell somebody about it. We could tell old Mitch Peterson's son. He's a detective." "And he's gonna laugh us right out the front door. You do realize that, don't you? We're gonna look like a couple of old senile fools . . . and in the end, nothing is going to come of it. Now, can you just shut up and drink your coffee?"

Robert blew out a quick breath and swigged from the off-white porcelain cup. The hot liquid slightly scorched his throat, and he hacked a bit.

They chatted for the next forty-five minutes and called it a morning. Usually, they sat around for an hour or more, but the morning's conversation had really heated up and Tim had no interest in addressing the issue and the remaining conversation had been forced. They talked about the heat and the humidity. Neither of them talked about their wives or the old days on the force, things that they normally conversed about.

Robert paid his tab at the front counter, left the diner and went home to his three-bedroom brick home on Pleasant Street, near Lincoln Park, on the north end of town. He sat back in his beat-up old recliner and read the newspaper article about the missing girl. His mind traveled back to a time that seemed like a lifetime ago.

Robert was in his fifties in 1980 and retirement had barely dropped into sight. There were many details about the case that Robert had forgotten, but there had always been one subject that had stuck out clearly in his mind: one of the gentlemen that had been interviewed. His name burned in the darkness of Robert's subconscious, but it would not come into the light. What was his name? Robert found that he was holding onto the edges of the newspaper so tight that he'd torn the pages. He folded the paper and set it down before walking to the kitchen.

Robert grabbed a soap-spotted glass from the cupboard and filled it with tap water. He hated bottled water and didn't see the point. The water from his tap had always been just fine and it tasted good too. Why would anyone spend money drinking what was most certainly just tap water in a fancy bottle?

What was his name?

Robert paced around the living room sipping from his glass. He stopped in front of the last Grabske family photo and traced the silver frame with his index finger. The photo had been taken in the early nineties, maybe ninety-two.

"Damn it! What was his name?" Robert finally said out loud, annoyed by his inability to come up with the name.

While Robert watched a few driblets of his water jump out from his glass and tumble to the floor, the name *Ted Olson* shot forward into his cerebral cortex. He whispered the name softly. "Ted Olson."

The interview with Ted came flooding back to him now like a tidal wave. The reception hall had been rented out to a young married couple. Robert had interviewed everyone invited to the wedding. Ted hadn't signed the guest list, and he hadn't been invited, but an old farmer who was also a mechanic on the side, had recognized him as a customer of his. It wasn't unusual for a local to drop by the bar of the reception hall. It remained open to the public. Apparently, Ted dropped his truck off at the farmer's house for repair on a few occasions. The farmer hadn't said anything to Ted. He really didn't know him that well, but somehow, he remembered that he'd been sitting at the bar.

Robert remembered his drive out to the interview with Ted who lived a few miles outside of Watertown in a house barely visible from the road. There had been loose gravel in the road, and upon further inspection he had found a gravel driveway just wide enough for his car to travel down, which led back into what—at first glance—appeared to be a field. He remembered the dank smell of the place. There was a sweet, smoky aroma that resonated around him as he stood in the driveway. The house was old, and it wasn't kept well. It could have been abandoned, which is not unusual in the back country of rural Wisconsin. At first, Robert hadn't thought much of Ted and his first impression was simple; Ted was just an old hermit that had stumbled upon the Jefferson House for a beer.

It was a bar.

As Robert stood in his own living room staring at a photo of Gina, he was amazed at how many details were coming back to him. He remembered the interview and what had been said. Ted had told Robert that he'd been in Milwaukee, looking for a place to live—that he was looking into some real estate, and had stopped by for a drink on his way home. It struck Robert as odd that a hermit like Ted would be in a city like Milwaukee looking for a place to live. The house that Ted lived in was old, far away from everything, but seemed to suit him. Judging by how cluttered everything was, it didn't click that Ted was planning to move anywhere, anytime soon. Robert remembered how cool and calculated Ted was with every answer he gave. At one point, Robert tried to shake Ted up a bit. Confuse him into saying something that conflicted with what he'd already said. But Ted had played the game and played it well. After the interview, Robert remembered asking flat out if Ted had killed those kids. And Ted had answered, no. But the way he'd answered was too cold. The man's nerves didn't twitch. There was something inhuman about Ted, and Robert knew it. In fact, he remembered feeling guilty for not having pursued Ted further. The interview stuck with Robert for a long time.

Robert realized that he was pacing again, and his hand was wrapped around his glass of water so tightly that his arthritic fingers ached. He set the glass down and went to his reclining chair, picked up the newspaper, and looked at the girl's photo again. Sadness washed over him. This was probably going to amount to nothing, but it bothered him badly. Robert hadn't felt this troubled since Gina had gotten sick.

How would he follow this up? Tim was right. If Robert were to go to the police station and explain his story, he'd be laughed right out the front door. But what could he do? There had to be something. He felt he needed to pursue this, even though a part of him was convinced that this was just one last attempt to do something meaningful with the remainder of his life. He found himself wondering what Gina would want him to do. He couldn't fathom that she would want him to sit tight. He hadn't been Eliot Ness in his days as a police officer, but he had enough instinct to know that this was more than just a coincidence. There were similarities here and a pattern to boot. So, what if Tim thought he was being stupid? If his hunch ended up being legitimate, then he would be able to sleep better knowing that he'd done the right thing. If he was wrong, then he would be a little embarrassed, but at his age he didn't care much about that.

Besides, he had time on his hands.

He didn't do much these days but wait to die.

Chapter 18
The Journal

1

Mary sat in her reclining chair in the living room, glancing over the daily newspaper. She wanted to cry, but she had no more tears. The skin around her eyes was red and itchy from rubbing away the tears. Jules had already been missing for nearly a week and reading about her disappearance in the newspaper, again, wasn't helping to ease her pain.

The community had been very supportive. The Benton's received numerous phone calls on a daily basis and in some ways, being around people helped diminish the sense of isolation that she and Richard both felt, but Mary was exhausted and wanted the phone calls to stop. She wanted the visitors to discontinue their visits, even though their gifts and condolences were appreciated. All she wanted was for her baby girl to come home. The sinking feeling that Mary felt in her stomach was more than she could handle. There was a lack of hope spreading like cancer within her. Her "mother's intuition" had already told her that she would never see her daughter again. Her emotional angst had peaked two days ago while she was sitting on the toilet. After releasing her bladder, she'd found that she couldn't stand up from the toilet seat. There was no strength left in her legs—they had quit her, and she felt hopeless. She wished that someone would just tell her that Jules was dead. Her worst nightmare was *not knowing* and the anxiety that followed stabbed at her weary mind with a thousand knives. Closure, whether it was good news or bad, was absolutely necessary at this point. She wanted the nightmare to be over with. The thought that Mary would rather know that Jules was dead than to live without knowing she was alive filled her heart with shame.

It had been days since she'd slept and even when brief moments of rest came to her, it had only been a half an hour here and there. Later in the day, Richard was going to take her to the doctor's office. She assumed that Doctor Horberg, a psychiatrist, would give her a prescription which would help her sleep. At this point, Mary didn't care what she took as long as it knocked her out for eight hours or more. She needed the escape from reality and her body and mind needed the rest. Whatever the doctor gave her, she hoped that it would knock her out so hard, and so fast, that she wouldn't dream. For if she had dreams, they would be of Jules and when she awoke, she would feel the crushing realization of her loss all over again. She didn't think she could handle that.

Richard was able to work. And in some respects, Mary could understand that. By putting his concentration into work, he was able to sidetrack his grief. When he came home, they barely talked. And if they did talk, it was very brief and to the point. At most, they would mindlessly babble about how so-and-so gave their sympathies for what had happened.

Detective Finley had called a few times. Mary found that she liked talking with him. He had a kind voice and he spoke to her without pity. She found herself thinking about him a lot as of recent, and not just because he was the detective on Jules' case. She needed male companionship, and she couldn't get it from Richard, not now.

The low rumble of Richard's truck pulling into the driveway shook Mary back to reality. The kitchen door creaked loudly as he came inside. "Mary! You home, babe?"

"Yes," she responded. She was annoyed by his question. He knew damn well that she was home, and he didn't need to ask.

She listened to him grunt and groan while he pulled off his work boots. He made his way into the living room, took a seat on the couch and turned on the television. They both stared at the flickering images, but neither of them got involved with the program. It was merely a distraction and ambient noise. After a few moments, Richard got up from the couch. "You want anything from the kitchen?"

"A glass of wine would be nice."

He nodded his head and made his way into the kitchen.

2

Richard's hands were achy and sore, especially in the meaty pocket where his thumb met the bottom part of his palm. When nervous, he would rub his hands together and knead his fingers deep into the soft tissue of his hands. Lately, he'd been kneading with too much strength and the pain had grown significantly.

In the kitchen, he stopped and listened, making sure that Mary wasn't getting up from her seat, and pulled down a bottle of Sky vodka from the top shelf of the pantry. He unscrewed the cap, put the bottle to his lips, and felt the icy rush of alcohol scorch down his throat. Until lately, he hadn't drunk straight alcohol. In fact, the bottle of Vodka was over a year old, and more than half full. It sent a soothing sense of calmness as it simmered his brain cells. He licked his lips and downed another long pull off the bottle. It felt good. He screwed the cap back on and pulled out a bottle of cabernet sauvignon from behind the vodka. He found two wine glasses and filled them nearly to the top, then carried them into the living room.

Mary was fixated on the television and didn't turn to look at him as he handed her the glass of crimson relaxation. He crossed the living room and sank into the couch. His wife had lost weight. She was depressed and not eating. She didn't look her best as of recent, but something about her damaged condition was strangely arousing. As unexplainable as the idea was, he had been feeling very frisky for her lately. Sexual feelings became heightened during times of stress, the need to know that one was still alive, and he assumed that's what was happening now. He wanted to take his wife into the bedroom and make love to her. Images of *taking her* started exploding in his mind. He drank the wine and set the empty glass down on the end table. When he met Mary's eyes and saw the way she was looking at him, his arousal heightened further.

Richard rose from the couch and went to her. He grabbed her hand and pulled her with him. They hustled down the hall and groped each other underneath the bedroom door frame. They kissed hard and vigorously. What they were doing, now, seemed more like a release of misplaced, animalistic aggression than an act of love.

Richard ripped Mary's button-down shirt off, grabbed her breast hard and squeezed. Her wine-stained breath smelled sweet and heavy. He pushed her onto the bed and pulled her pants off fast. She was wearing a black thong. Richard took the rest of his clothes off, grabbed her knees with his aching hands and spread her legs apart. He hadn't been this turned-on since he was much younger. She was moaning loudly, and she grabbed his arms, pulling him upward. Their lips met and he entered her, thrusting into her hard. A short time later they fell into the bed together and caught their breath.

3

Mary felt a surge of guilt erupt from within her. Crying hard and loud, she wailed into her pillow. She reached over and wrapped her arms around Richard. The warmth of his chest was comforting. "I miss her so much. I don't know if I can do this!" She started convulsing, and her stomach muscles were strained and sore. It felt good to weep.

4

Richard hadn't loved his wife this intensely in many years. He wanted to ease her pain, but he was helpless to do so. In this moment, Richard and Mary renewed their love and acknowledged that it was genuine and special. Although they were dealing with the worst of all nightmares, Richard conceded that he and his wife could survive these horrible times if they could simply console one another. This devastation was a milestone in their journey together. Through true intimacy and love they could dig hard and pull through this dark passage. Mary began trembling, and he pulled the sheets up over her naked body.

At least he could shield her from the cold.

Mary was asleep within minutes. She had a doctor's appointment at six-thirty, which was in fifteen minutes, so Richard called Doctor Horberg and canceled. This was the first time in days that Mary had been able to fall into a deep slumber and Richard would be damned if he'd ruin her state of rest. Doctor Horberg was kind enough to reschedule for the following day at six-thirty.

After putting on his robe, Richard crept down the hallway toward Jules' room. He stopped and focused on her closed door.

Looking down at the space between the hardwood floor and the bottom of the door, Richard hoped to see a passing shadow. That somehow, he was the one asleep, not Mary, and that the past week had been a nightmare, and Jules was safe at home. *She wasn't.* He twisted the knob and entered Jules' room.

The first thing that swam into his thoughts like a nostalgic parade was her scent. It was faint, but it was pleasant, and it was everywhere. It was in the air, in the sheets of her bed, and in her clothes. Richard went to her closet and ruffled through her sweaters and her shirts. He felt the living presence of his daughter and it was good. He went to her bed and could almost envision her beautiful smell rising from the sheets as he sat down on top of them. The cotton fabric was cold, but it was comforting, and Richard leaned back, flattening out on the queen-sized mattress.

He looked up at the ceiling and an odd realization struck him. The thought was nothing really, but it was everything. He had never been in Jules' room, looking up at the ceiling, as he supposed she did every night in her bed. His eyes washed over every imperfection of the ceiling, and he wondered if Jules had noticed the same things that he did. Really, there was nothing except cracked paint. Besides the fact that her room was in need of a few coats of paint, the room was nice. Richard was glad that he could see what his daughter saw. These last few minutes had temporarily filled his void. For the first time since Jules had disappeared, he found himself thanking God with prayer.

After a few more minutes, Richard became used to the faint feminine scent of Jules, and he lost her smell. He rolled over, sat up, and felt a slight hump beneath the mattress. Turning toward the middle of the bed, he began smoothing over it with the palm of his hand, fingers extended. He felt something as he slid his hand from the bottom of the bed to the top. He hopped off the mattress, squatted down, and pried it up above his head. The comforter slid halfway to the floor and bundled near the base. His hands started to ache again, and he realized that he was straining to hold the mattress up. It was hard to see anything in the dark, but then he saw something small and thin wedged about two feet under the mattress. He stretched his back muscles and reached for the object. It felt heavy and loose. After his fingers fluttered through it, he realized that it was a book of some kind. His fingers stretched further, grasped the edge, and slid it forward. He pulled it out and let the mattress fall back onto the box spring. It crashed loudly into place and Richard spun around toward the door, hoping that the noise hadn't woken Mary. He stood still and silent. Curiosity overwhelmed him while he glanced over the book. He opened it.

In the dark, all Richard could see was hand-scribble. *The book was a journal*. He flipped through the first few pages and went to switch the light on. He looked down the hallway toward the master bedroom and didn't see Mary, which was a good thing. He closed the door, sat down on the bed and opened the journal to the first page. His heart was thumping in his chest.

5

January 6th, 2010

David Miller sits next to me in second period American History. I've known of him for a long time, but I've never really talked to him until now, I mean we've been in school together since kindergarten, we just never clicked, I guess. He is very skinny, which I don't like much, but when he smiles at me, I get a tingly feeling all over. Every morning when I get to class, he goes out of his way to ask me how I'm doing and then he scurries back to his seat so that he won't get yelled at by Mrs. Mullen. Lately, I've had the urge to just walk over to him and kiss him. I'd never actually do that, but I think about it. His lips are big and full, and he has a really nice smile. His face gets all red when he speaks to me and I think that, maybe, he feels the same way about me that I feel about him. I hope he does. Well, thanks for listening, diary. This is why I love you so much, I can tell you everything and I know you won't judge me or tell anyone. You're the best therapy a girl could ask for.

February 25th, 2010

I saw David at Penny's party on Friday night, and we kissed. He was a bit tipsy, but it was nice. I think he only got drunk so that he could work up his nerve. I don't think I've ever been so nervous in my life, but it felt great to have his lips pressed up against mine. It was everything that I imagined, and I want more. At the end of the night, before Penny drove me home, he told me that we could go on a real date next Saturday. I don't know how my dad will feel about that, but I don't care because I really like him. Penny thinks that I can do better. She says that David's really not that cute, but to me he's gorgeous. I hope that our date goes well.

6

Richard slapped the journal shut, clenching the cover tightly in his hands. Reading through the history of how Jules and David became a couple was sickening, and while going through her diary was definitely invading her privacy, it didn't matter because there might be something written within these pages that could shed light on what may or may not have happened to her. Richard set the journal down next to him, spread his arms wide, and forced his knuckles into the tissue on both sides of his spine in an attempt to crack his back. There were a few pops and cracks, which relaxed him. He picked up the book and reopened it. Looking down at his daughter's handwriting, he realized that this diary was her most intimate friend and if she was open and honest with the book, then maybe the book could give an open and honest hint as to where she might be.

Richard assumed that he was not going to enjoy what he might find within these cheap white pages, but he might find something; maybe a lead. He turned to the second page of the journal and continued reading.

Most of the book's content was mindless babble about school, gossip and disagreements with Richard, but the words were his daughter's honest thoughts and feelings and he suddenly felt closer to his daughter. If what was written in these pages were true, then he imagined that he and his wife were doing a fairly decent job of raising her. According to this, she didn't drink much—even with a best friend like Penny Sloan, who Richard really never cared for much. She just didn't seem like a nice girl. Richard always thought of Penny as the bad apple, the friend that would influence Jules into her first cigarette, her first drink, and probably her first puff of a joint.

With eagerness bubbling in his blood, Richard continued to read.

For many of the pages, Jules came across as the above average teenage girl. In fact, Richard was glad to see that he hadn't created as much angst for her as he thought he may have. The entries that pertained to him were good. There were a few sections where she went on about how unfair he'd been, but then she would write about how she understood his logic. Like the time she and Penny had been caught skipping school. He'd grounded her for two weeks. Richard remembered those two weeks vividly because Jules had been a menace the entire time. At the time, he didn't know who was being punished more; Jules or him. There were a few times that Richard stopped reading and thought about how nicely crafted Jules' sentences were. She may have had . . . may have . . . a future in writing. Then sadness and anger came back to him, and he continued to read for clues. If there was one thing that Richard had been right about, it was that David wasn't good enough for Jules and it was written between the lines of her journal.

Then Richard got to the entry that stabbed him through the heart.

7

March 1st, 2010

David and I have talked about having sex and we've decided that we're going to do it. His parents are going out of town later this month and both David and I agree that this would be the ideal opportunity for us. I'm scared and nervous and excited all at once. We talked about all the details—he is going to bring protection. I kind of feel guilty because I don't know if I should be doing this or not. My father is always preaching to me about how I should wait until I'm married, but I don't believe people do that anymore. I feel right about this. I think that I love David, although I would never tell him that, not yet anyway. I hope it turns out to be everything that I imagined it to be. I've talked with Penny—she's done it a lot—and she says that it isn't magical or anything. She says that the first time is rather bad and that it hurts. I hope it doesn't hurt because I want it to be special. I think that everyone hopes their first time is special, but I mean it. I think David is different than other boys too because he is respectful of my feelings. He listens to what I have to say, and we planned everything like adults do.

March 7th, 2010

David and I made love last night and it was wonderful. It didn't happen exactly as I had imagined, but it was amazing, nonetheless. Even though I haven't told David yet, I love him. The whole night was fantastic, David's parents were gone up north and he made me dinner, which we didn't eat. We went straight to the bedroom. We were both so nervous at first, but then it happened, and it was like nothing I'd ever felt before. It was so amazing, and it didn't hurt as bad as Penny said it would. There was a little sting at first, but I told David about it, and he eased up. He was nice, slow, and gentle. Everything about David is perfect, I wouldn't change a thing. Although I feel bad about lying to my father, I feel right about what David and I did. Still, I didn't tell my dad that David's parents were gone. I don't think that he would have allowed me out of the house if he had known.

Besides that, everything went perfect. Oh, except that David forgot to buy condoms, but he pulled out—I know that sounds so irresponsible, but I think that we should be all right. I just pray that he loves me back.

I couldn't help but feel a little bit guilty after it happened. I know that I'm not supposed to have sex until I'm ready, or married, if you ask my dad, but it felt so right. And anyhow, when does anybody really know that they're ready? My life has never felt so complete and I'm hoping that David and I will be together forever, maybe even go to the same college after we graduate. I guess time will tell.

8

Richard had to close the journal, feeling sick to his stomach after what he'd just read. The book suddenly seemed to weigh a ton. His arms were fatigued, and he almost set it down, but he couldn't. It was important that he read every sentence. He thought that maybe the story would lead his suspicions somewhere, maybe even answer the question: where is Jules? After taking a deep breath, he looked to the small round Kitty Clock above the door frame and saw that it was ten o'clock. He'd been in Jules' room for over three hours groveling over his daughter's written words. After rubbing his dry eyes, he turned back to the neat scribbling in the ledger.

9

April 20th, 2010

I've been sick to my stomach every morning for the past week. The sickness isn't that bad in the afternoon or at night, but in the mornings, I can't help throwing up. I must have caught that strain of the flu going around. I heard that a few girls at school had caught it. Anyway, I'm sure it's nothing that a bottle of Echinacea won't fix.

April 25th, 2010

I am pregnant. I took three pregnancy tests and then went to Planned Parenthood to confirm. I can't believe this is happening to me. My dad is probably going to disown me, and I feel like the biggest slut on the planet. I can't see myself getting rid of the baby either. I just couldn't do that. I don't know what to do and I feel so lost that I don't know if I'll ever find my way again. I am so stupid for not making David use protection. In fact, I'm sure that this is God's way of punishing me for the sins that I've committed—dad was right. I guess all I can do is take it day by day. I think that I'm going to tell David after the spring formal. I hope that we can have this baby and do everything together, although I don't think that David would have a problem going through with an abortion. I can't.

10

Richard was beginning to think that maybe Jules had indeed run away from home. It was true, if she were to have told him she was pregnant, he probably would have given her the third degree. He'd always preached to her that sex before marriage was a sin; and even though he and Mary had been having sex since well before they were married—some of their best sexual experiences had taken place before their vows—he started to think that Jules was scared, and that she was hiding out someplace. Maybe she was at a friend's house and didn't realize the severity of what was happening. Right now, he just wanted her home so that they could deal with the situation as a family. If she came home, he would not yell at her or punish her, he would only support her. His eyes watered up. He would be a grandfather. It was a gift.

Richard looked at the clock. It was one o'clock in the morning. The police station was still open—obviously—but he wasn't sure that he should call them just yet. He would wait until tomorrow to give this new information to that detective. *What was his name? Finley.* It was late and Richard didn't know how he wanted to present this information to the police. He would call Detective Finley in the morning and tell him what he had discovered.

Richard couldn't explain why, but he lifted the mattress and replaced the journal where he had found it, then made the bed, nice and tight. He looked at the walls, at all the photos of Jules' friends that were stuffed into the creases of the vanity mirror above her dresser and realized that he had learned more about his daughter's life in the few hours that he'd snooped through her belongings than he had from years of attempting to converse with her. One photo on the mirror stuck out in particular, of Jules and David standing together at a party. David had a smirk on his face and must have been staring directly into the camera lens because Richard could feel his gaze. He took the photo down. Holding it gently between his fingers, he studied the composition of the picture and for one brief moment he felt as though he were having a staring contest with David, via the photograph. He didn't like the way David smiled. There was something smug and maniacal about the way his lips curled up at the corners of his mouth.

Richard's mind began to race when he remembered the entry in Jules' journal. She was going to tell David about the pregnancy after the dance. Had she already told him? What did David do? Did he take her someplace to hide out? The idea that two high school kids would hide out during a pregnancy suddenly felt silly, especially for someone as mature as Jules.

He crumpled the picture and his anger stewed. He whispered, "What did you do to my daughter?"

11

The next morning Mary woke up and smiled, totally refreshed. Then her smile fell, and a strange sort of paleness took her color, and she appeared sick. As if a moment of happiness after a long night's sleep was wrong, she forced guilt upon herself and said, "I can't be happy while my angel is gone."

Richard pulled her into his chest and held her. His eyes felt dry and they were red with exhaustion. After going through Jules' diary and learning about the last few months of her life, he had not been able to sleep well. He'd lain in bed and took solace in watching Mary sleep for the first time in days. He weighed his options heavily through the restless night. What he should have done was call the police and let them know what he had discovered. That was the right thing to do—that and tell his wife.

Richard climbed out of bed and went to the bathroom. He could see Mary moving around on the bed as he looked at her from the reflection in the small mirror above the bathroom sink. She was dumping pills into her hand. They were probably Xanax. She'd been taking them for the past few days. It was surprising to Richard that she wasn't able to sleep, given the amount of anxiety medication she was taking. He finished peeing and walked out of the bathroom.

"Do you want coffee?"

"I'll have a cup," Mary responded.

In the kitchen Richard dumped cheap coffee grounds into the coffeemaker. All coffee tasted the same to Richard and the only reason he drank it was for the caffeine. He had never actually admired the taste of it. It was hot and bitter with a bit of a kick. After he started the coffee, he took a seat at the kitchen table. The sound of the hot water bubbling with the morning wake-up-juice floated into his ears. He was tired, yet fully awake, and was still debating his options. He would call the police and tell the detective about the journal, the pregnancy, and he would let the law officials take care of what needed to be done. That was the only logical option. But then the cold sting of logic simmered down, and he thought about what *he could do*. What would be best for his family? Maybe he would hold off telling Mary about the journal for a day or two. And he could do a little investigating of his own. He looked at the clock and saw that it was six. He thought about calling in sick. His boss would understand. They'd been asking him to take a few days off for the past week. They wanted him to stay home and be with his family, his wife. He went to the phone and dialed work.

Bill Henniger, the general manager at the bottling factory, answered the phone. "Hey Bill, Richard Benton here, look . . . I think it might be best if I stayed home with Mary today."

"Richard, say no more. Take a couple days off and sort things out. I won't even take it out of your sick days," Bill answered.

"Thanks Bill, I really appreciate it." Richard hung up the phone, wondering why he had just called in sick. What did he *really* intend to do?

Mary was still lying in bed. He put on his work shirt and pants, leaned down and kissed her quickly. "I have to go to work now, babe," he lied.

As if he were being directed by a higher power, Richard found himself driving through town, avoiding Main Street and ended up parked across the street from David Miller's house. He sat in his truck and watched the house as if it were going to move. At about seven-twenty, David finally walked out the front door and shuffled across the walkway to his car. He opened the car door, got in, and pulled out of the driveway. Richard started his truck and followed David from a distance. He was probably just going to school, since that's what most teens did on Tuesday mornings during the school year. They drove up Water Street and made a right onto Endeavour Drive. David parked toward the back of the school lot and sat in his car for a long while.

Richard parked in the corner of the lot opposite David, and observed, watching him sit in his car while the last of the students scurried into the building. The school bell rang loud and echoed through the parking lot. And still, David remained in his car.

Another five minutes passed, and Richard began to wonder whether David was going to attend school or not. Was it destiny that he had called in sick for work? Richard started to ask himself what was happening, if everything taking place was some sort of destined intervention. Richard's attention was drawn to the sound of David's car starting up.

David lowered his head and put the car into drive. Panic took Richard when he realized that David was driving slowly in his direction. He slumped down low in the seat until he felt that his head was hidden from sight. For a minute, Richard thought for sure David would recognize his truck, walk up to him, and ask what he was doing.

That didn't happen.

David's car rumbled past, and Richard found himself slowly peeking over the steering wheel, out the window. David was headed out the rear entrance and driving toward County Trunk A, which led out of town.

Richard's curiosity got the best of him, and he followed David out into the country. He remained a good distance behind David's Honda. He was certain that David would not be able to identify his truck. There was too much distance between them. The sun shined brightly through the windshield and stabbed at Richard's sensitive eyes. He should have brought his sunglasses. At one point, the sun shone so brightly that he lost track of how close the gap was sinking between he and David—only a hundred feet. He tapped the brakes to regain his distance.

About five miles outside of town, David pulled into The Garden wildlife reserve. Richard hadn't been there in many years. It would probably end up being a school ditch-party, but all the same Richard wanted to know what he was up to.

Richard allowed David a minute to pull ahead into the woods. He followed slowly down the gravel path into the shade of the trees. If memory served him correctly, they were headed toward a small lake.

From a few hundred feet, Richard could see David's car parked next to the water's edge. He stopped the truck, put it in reverse, and drove slowly back toward the entrance. A small dirt path caught his eye, and he cranked the wheel to the left. Once he was far enough back in a small clearing, he killed the engine. He hoped that he could locate David. He heard the faint ripple of splashing water, and he followed the sound.

Richard found David by accident. He was turned around in the woods and was about to give up looking when, suddenly, the echo of David's voice drifted through the morning breeze. Although he was only whispering, the sound carried a long way in the stillness of the forest.

Richard quickly, but silently, crept toward David.

Richard was dangerously close. His vision was limited, but he could see David between the trees. And saw enough of him to know that he was sitting down against the trunk of a large elm tree. He was picking at something in his hands, maybe the leaves off a small branch. Or maybe he was picking at a scab. Even from this distance Richard could see that David's hands were swollen and injured. He fought the urge to breathe heavy. He could only imagine what would happen if David spotted him. He wiped the back of his hand across his face. It came back sopping wet with sweat. Looking down at his work clothes, he was surprised by how soaked he'd become. Placing his hand to his chest, he felt the heavy throb of his heartbeat, and the blood pumping through his chest. Lowering himself onto his hands and knees, he crawled behind a thicket of brush and twigs, and settled.

David was clear in Richard's vision now. Once he concentrated, Richard could hear what David was saying. *Why was he talking to himself?* Richard's heart silently exploded into a million pieces. David was looking at a loose mound of fresh dirt, piled over something that had been buried underneath. Richard slowly lifted his hand, placed his knuckles between his teeth, and bit down hard. He didn't know what was stopping him from rushing over to David and snapping his neck, but he needed to listen like he'd needed to read Jules' diary. No matter how bad it was, he needed to find out what had happened. But in his heart, his mind, and in his bones, Richard Benton knew what was buried in front of David.

Richard's soul seemed to leave him, and he slumped down onto his butt and leaned against the brush that concealed him. He needed to hear what David was saying. In horrified silence, Richard continued to listen to David's slow monotone voice while he spoke to the mound of fresh dirt.

"This is probably stupid . . . coming here when I know I could get caught, but I had to, Jules. I had to come and talk to you. I owe you that much. I owe you more than that, actually, and that's why I'm here. What I did was an act of madness. It was crazy. I don't know what came over me . . . and I don't know what came over me again when I . . ." He pointed at the grave and, in the air, traced the outline of the mound with his index finger. Blood dripped from the palm of his hand. "I buried you out here like some kind of animal. I couldn't handle having a baby, Jules. I thought that by having a baby it would end my life. God I'm stupid . . . stupid, Jules, stupid. I acted out on the first impulse that rang through my stupid head and now look at the mess I'm in. A cop came and visited me the other day . . . asked me a bunch of questions. I'm lucky he didn't arrest me on the spot . . . and it's not like they're not going to find out what happened. My parents are up my ass too and I can tell by the way they look at me, that they know I did it. I came out here, today, to tell you that I'm turning myself in. I'll tell the police where you are, and I'll take my sentence." He fell forward to his knees and hugged the mound of dirt, sobbing loud and crying out. "I fucked up so bad, Jules. If I could trade places with you . . . God knows I would." He was silent as he lay down against the earth.

Richard could feel his eyeballs pushing forward as if they wanted to pop out of his head. The anger he felt was maddening. He wanted to kill him. He didn't want David to turn himself in. He wanted to serve justice with his own hand. Looking to the sky, he asked God "Why?" Why had he taken his daughter from him? He had been such a good servant and strived to be the best person he could be, and he took the Good Book seriously. *This was the thanks that he received?* His daughter was dead and discarded like a piece of trash. How could God let something like this happen to one of his precious children? He remained frozen while David sobbed next to his daughter's grave. A whirlwind of awfulness swirled violently through Richard's weary mind.

It took a long time for Richard to calm down. David was silent now and his face was red and swollen. His chest rose and fell with quick breaths. Finally, David stood up and stepped back. Richard quickly flopped over onto his stomach and observed. The leaves crackled beneath him and when he looked out, David seemed to be staring in Richard's direction. Then his gaze fell below Richard.

David was fumbling and seemed nervous. His eyes were wide and his fingers fidgety. When he took another step back, he fell to the ground, then quickly sprung to his feet. Richard tucked back into a gathering of foliage and continued to wait.

David sat and stared at Jules' grave. About five minutes later he slowly walked away with a blank face, but not before expressing his final comments to Jules. "I'm so sorry, Jules. I promise you that I will turn myself in on Friday and put closure to everyone's worry. I'm sure that it won't cure the hurt I've caused, but at least the truth will be told. It's Tuesday today. I just want a couple of days to say goodbye and take care of the things that I need to take care of." And with that, David left.

Richard stayed quiet and watched David head back to his car. After a few minutes, Richard stood up from his hiding place and slowly stumbled over to Jules' grave. Tears were streaming from his eyes and spilling onto his filthy work shirt, making the dirt spots thicken into mud. He fell to his knees in front of the small mound of dirt, which was about five feet long and he had no idea how deep. Richard turned to the side and vomited when he smelled the rot of his daughter seeping up from beneath the soil. David must not have buried Jules deep enough. Richard stuck his fingers into the dirt and felt how loose it was. While wiping the vomit from his mouth, he thought about digging her up. He wanted to see her, even if she was dead. He needed closure.

David's confession had been more than enough to confirm his suspicions. Still—he needed this.

He started to push the dirt off to the side. He stopped, rolled back against the tree trunk that David had been resting against, let his head fall back, and looked up at the green leaves and the dark branches of the tree. Little shimmers of light shot through the branches while he looked to the sky. The tree trunk was warm where David had sat against it and suddenly Richard hated the warmth. He looked at the grave and for the first time in days, he thought clearly. What he was thinking seemed logical, even though the notion was insane. He would kill David. He would take justice for his daughter's demise. Mary needed to know what had happened too. And he would tell her. If he were to leave The Garden and go to the police, he was certain that David would be arrested and convicted as an adult. He would spend ten years—or more—in prison, then he would return to society. He might even come back to Watertown. Richard and his wife would protest. And no one would welcome David back. Still, he would be free, his debt to society paid.

Not on my watch!

Richard stood, turned to the sky and shook his fist. "What about the justice she deserves! What about Jules? It isn't enough!" His fist continued to shake along with his body before he leaned over and hyperventilated. When he finally grasped onto the rhythm of his breathing again, he looked at his watch and realized that he needed to go. There was much to think about and to be planned. And what had David said? He would turn himself in on

Friday. That only gave Richard a few days to carry out his plan—the plan he hadn't thought of yet.

Mary would lose it. She would go insane, no matter how he delivered the news. Her only child—that she loved more than her own life—had been stolen and discarded. He needed to tell her quick—he needed to get her approval for what must be done. But she would never go for it. Asking his wife if it was okay to murder their daughter's killer was not domestic conversation that took place between two consenting adults. She would say *no* because that was the right thing to say. She would want to go to the police, turn David in and watch the legal mess unfold. But that was logical thinking, and this situation was not logical. When one becomes the victim, logic is sent out the window.

It was hard to concentrate on the road while Richard drove home from The Garden. His torment was distracting, and, like a drunkard, he found himself swerving off the road more than once. All he could think about was Jules. For reasons unknown, he was recalling Christmases when she was no more than three feet tall and a brat, but she was precious. He remembered watching her open her presents and thinking to himself that he would never let anything happen to her; no one would ever touch a hair on her gentle head. He would guard her from the horrors of life.

A lot of good he was.

The worst thing in the world had happened to her and he hadn't protected her from shit—not a fucking thing. He was a failure to his family. The one thing that a man must protect most in the world is his children and he had failed. From the beginning, he didn't like David—thought he was bad news. In his heart, he knew that David was an infection to Jules. Yet he let her go out with him, and even respected him when he picked her up for that stupid dance. Now his baby was dead and rotting in a cold unmarked grave in the woods, with her own child.

The one positive piece of information was that he knew— he knew what had happened and there was a small window of opportunity to do something about it.

Chapter 19
Acting On Suspicion

1

Robert Grabske parked his car across the street from the Watertown Police Department and wobbled to the crosswalk. He looked with nostalga over at the stationhouse. It had changed drastically since he'd retired. When he served as a policeman the brick building was a cream color; it was nice, but had a punishing look about it. It looked like a building that you wouldn't want to enter. It gave, even the common man, a feeling of guilt as he walked up the concrete steps and entered the tinted glass doors that led into the lobby, which housed orange plastic chairs bolted to the wall. Now, the brick was red and more inviting—the place seemed built for comfort. Disagreeing with the remodeling choice, Robert shook his head and walked across the street.

The front doors were still made of thick tinted glass, but the lobby had changed. The chairs were now padded with blue cushions and the end tables were covered with magazines and current newspapers. There was still a bit of graffiti scribbled on the walls, but it wasn't as bad as when he had left the force. Back then, the lobby walls had been badly desecrated, violent murals.

Robert stumbled over to the dispatcher sitting behind the bullet-proof glass window, drinking her coffee. He rang the service bell and asked, "Since when did they start hiring pretty girls to run the dispatch?"

"Do you have a complaint sir?" she asked with a cold voice.

"Well, not so much a complaint. Say, is there a detective on duty?" he asked.

"Let me see." She leaned over a microphone, pushed a small red button at the base of it, and spoke into the receiver.

Robert could hear her voice echoing behind the lobby walls. If his memory served correctly, immediately behind the wall was a vast maze of cubicle offices and cheap metal desks set up for the detectives. Off to the right were the glass-encased offices where the captain and chief resided and conducted their business. And in back of the offices were six standard, small town jail cells. Now, Robert imagined that everything looked much different.

The dispatcher turned a blank eye to Robert. "They're all busy at the moment. Is this an emergency?"

It might be an emergency, or it might be a waste of time, Robert didn't really know. "I suppose it isn't. No, it's not an emergency," he replied. He was starting to feel like a paranoid and senile bastard about to make a complaint over what would turn out to be nothing.

"Just have a seat and a detective will be with you as soon as possible," the dispatcher said, nodding slowly to make sure that he understood.

Robert took his seat, unhappy about the way things were going. In his mind, he had hoped that when he entered the station, someone would recognize him, bring him into the office and provide him with the VIP treatment. But no, he was just another annoying civilian that these small-town cops didn't feel like spending their energy on. The sad fact was that he understood. He couldn't come close to remembering all the times he'd avoided old folks like himself. When the elderly came in with a complaint, he would make sure that there wasn't a real emergency and tend to that person when it became convenient. Sometimes, they would wait so long and simply leave, and he would write the incident off as unimportant.

After reading pages one through five of the Watertown Daily Times, Robert stood and glanced over to the dispatch woman who pretended that she didn't see him. Unsatisfied and humiliated, Robert stood, walked to the exit, and pushed the door open as hard as he could, trying to draw a rise out of dispatch. The door was heavy, and it almost knocked him to the floor. After stumbling backward, he gained control of his balance, left the station, stumbled across the street to his car, and drove away.

If he took a right on Milford Street and hit One Mile Road, took a left, and drove for three or four miles, he might come out by the house where he thought that Ted lived. He would just drop in and make small talk. Maybe he still had a little police sense left in him. After all these years, he didn't think that Ted would recognize him. Hell, it had been twenty-nine years since they'd *last* seen each other and that was also the *first time* they'd ever seen each other. What could it hurt? If nothing else, it would prove that he was wrong.

As he neared the stretch of desolate road that he believed Ted lived on, he realized he had no idea how he was going to kick off the conversation. What would he talk about? It didn't seem right to just knock on the door and ask Ted if he'd heard about the girl that went missing from the Jefferson House. That wouldn't work. The answer didn't come to him, but he didn't care. He was determined and if his instincts served him correctly, maybe he could just take one look at the man and know if he was a killer. A killer has a look about him. His eyes aren't quite focused on what you're saying or what you're doing. Robert assumed that what happened behind the eyes of a killer was something much different. Everything perceived by them was a perverted truth. Their souls were painted black, and it reflected through the coldness of their eyes. Many of Robert's colleagues thought his philosophical theories on killers were nonsense. But his instincts seemed accurate, at least partially, to him. And he believed in them.

The road was empty and there didn't seem to be a driveway in sight. But then he recalled the last time he'd driven this route. The house had been hard to find back then, and it was hard to find now. What he remembered from twenty-nine years ago was the scattered gravel that sprinkled out from the driveway.

And then it appeared in front of him. Two tire paths that lengthened toward a wide clearing further up into what looked like a field, at first glance. Robert parked his car, looked into the foliage and saw the weather-beaten wood siding. Fear, twisted with excitement, tingled through Robert's bloodstream as he pulled the steering wheel to the left and drove up the path.

2

Ted sat quietly in the kitchen, sipping on a cup of very strong coffee. The first sip was always the best; more so because of the initial rush of caffeine punching his system than for the flavor. Ted wasn't big on taste or flavor when it came to food and drink. He looked out the window and saw an older model blue Buick coming up the driveway. Shooting up from his seat, Ted's chair slid back about three feet and nearly tumbled over. He crept up next to the window frame, peeled back the thin curtain and peered outside. The car slowed, then stopped near the barn. An old man stepped out of the car. Ted chuckled. If anyone were to get lost out here, it would be an old man. No one ever saw the driveway from the road. That was Ted's intention. The old buzzard probably got lost and pulled off to the side of the road. Something probably caught his eye. And that something was his house, or the barn.

The old man squinted, put his hand over the top of his eyes, as if saluting, and inspected the property. Ted shook his head. He thought about killing the old-timer, but there was no sport in it. Killing the old man would be a waste of a score. Ted walked down the short hallway between the kitchen and front door. The hallway was cluttered with old, yellow cardboard boxes filled with newspapers, silverware, and random knick-knacks that had been there for nearly thirty years, maybe more.

Ted opened the cheap wooden door and lifted up on the screen handle. The old man was standing on the porch and looked lost. Something felt oddly familiar to Ted about this old man, as if he knew him. It couldn't be. The only people Ted knew were his scores. "You need help old man? I don't have a phone, never have."

The old man rested his hand on the wooden rail that started at the bottom of the steps and ran the length of his porch. For a moment, Ted thought to tell the old man that the railing was no good and that if he leaned on it too hard, he might fall. If he did fall, Ted thought that he would probably have to kill him. It would save the trouble of getting him to a hospital. Chances were no one knew that the old man had come out this way. The house wasn't even listed in the phone directory. Ted had bought a telephone book a few years back and read through it, just to make sure. Except for the small disability and social security checks that he received at a post office box, no one knew that he lived near town. He'd been pleased to see there was no listing for a "Ted Olson." For a quick second, Ted thought that maybe this guy was an old friend from the Marine Corps. The only *beings* that he would ever associate as friends were the ones he'd met in service.

"No trouble, I was just stopping in. Saw your house from the road and wanted to see if anyone lived here," the old man said and then seemed to force a smile.

There was something cocky about the old man's smile that Ted didn't like and suddenly the familiarity of this man grew stronger. "Do I know you, old man?"

The old man shook his head. "No, I was just kind of . . . exploring. You live out here by yourself?"

Now Ted was starting to feel the flame of anger boiling in his stomach. He didn't like being questioned and he especially didn't like to be questioned about his nest. Ted stepped out onto the porch and let the screen door slam shut behind him. "What's your business fellow?"

The strange old man started waving his hands at chest level, as if in surrender, and began to chuckle again. "I didn't mean to bother you. I'm sorry. Please, I'm just trying to make conversation. I'm retired. I spend a lot of time driving around . . . out here . . . on the back roads. You mind chatting with me for a spell?"

Ted looked back at his house and thought for a minute. He'd never anticipated something like this. But he believed the old-timer and it might be best to humor him for a half an hour or so, then let him be on his way. As old as this man looked, he probably wouldn't remember how he'd found the place once he left. "Sure, come on inside." Ted lifted the screen door handle to let the old man inside.

3

Robert was amazed at how quickly and smoothly he had gained entry into Ted's house. Still, there was also a very frightening feeling that he was walking into the lion's den. When Ted had stepped out onto the porch, Robert froze with fear. For a moment, he could have sworn that Ted recognized him. But his "senile-old-man-trick" had worked, and now he was inside the house.

The house smelled strange. Not necessarily bad, but the
air was stale and a sweet-metallic odor permeated the walls, which were covered with peeling wallpaper and there was a yellowish tint to almost everything including the ceiling. This man was a hermit and probably didn't have a wife. At least he didn't have one back in 1980.

The wood floor creaked with each step that Robert took, heightening his paranoia. He had to remind himself that he was undercover. Well, he didn't know if "undercover" was a term that applied to vigilantism, and he still didn't fully understand why he was here. He *did* know that finding Ted was the result of some strange sort of destiny. He wanted to find out if this man had anything to do with the disappearance of this latest girl. Robert knew, in his bones, that he did. Most killers only got better and more organized with experience. If Robert had access to police resources, he probably could have found some sort of pattern, somewhere.

"I just brewed a fresh pot of coffee. You want a cup?" Ted asked without turning around to make eye contact.

Robert suddenly felt like turning around and leaving, as fast as he possibly could. Intuition was alerting him that something was amiss here. "Sure. That would be real nice," Robert said. He was surprised that he didn't sound nervous.

"How long have you lived here?"

4

There he was, asking questions again. Ted was beginning to grow sour with the old man's visit. There was something suspicious happening. Then, he shook off the notion as paranoia and entered the kitchen. He retrieved an off-white mug from the cupboard and poured hot black coffee into it.

"I don't carry cream or sugar."

"Black is fine," the old man said.

"What's your name?" Ted asked.

Maybe a name would ring a bell?

The old man hesitated.

Ted felt the cold rush of his nerves skittering up his spine. Through his peripheral vision, Ted could see the old man's lips quivering and he felt that something was definitely wrong.

"Bob. Bob is my name," the old man finally said.

Bob. He didn't know anyone named Bob.

"Well, have a seat at the table . . . Bob," Ted ordered.

The old man, Bob, turned in circles, settled, then pulled a chair out from the table and plopped down into it. Ted set a mug down in front of him.

5

Robert felt like he was in some kind of zone. His mind was hazy. Ted must have known that something was amiss when he hesitated before telling Ted his name—a fake name. Well, actually, he hadn't lied since Bob was short for Robert.

Ted was handing Robert his mug of coffee. "It's hot."

"That's fine. I like a kick in my coffee," Robert answered.

Ted took a seat across the table from him and crossed his legs. "So, you drive around out this way often?" Ted asked, sipping his cup of coffee.

Robert drank from the mug and immediately winced from the bitter potency of it. He set the cup down and pretended to agree with the flavor. When he looked to Ted, there seemed to be a menacing grin planted across his face.

"It's a bit tough, I know. I don't usually have guests," Ted said. He took a quick look out the small window above the sink. "And if I do, they don't usually stay long." Ted laughed out loud.

"You have family here, Ted? In Watertown, I mean?" Robert found himself asking. He was forcing conversation. And he was pretty sure that Ted could sense a deeper reason for his visit.

Ted shrugged his shoulders and curled his lip. "No . . . not anymore. I'm out here by myself. I've been by myself for a long time. I like it, it's peaceful."

"I imagine it would be," Robert said, sitting up in his chair. He could feel his cheeks begin to burn. There had been numerous times that he'd become flushed and nervous during the course of his career in law enforcement. Usually right before he asked the million-dollar question. And then it came to him. "You hear about that girl that went missing?"

There was a long silence as Ted uncrossed then crossed his legs. He put his finger to his forehead and seemed to be pondering. Robert had never felt so nervous in all his life. The room felt like it was closing in on him. He was in the lion's den and had kept it tame . . . until now.

6

Bob's demeanor had deceived Ted, but now he saw clearly. His thin lips stretched across his face and a familiar rush of blood pulsated through his body. It was like watching a mouse inching closer and closer to a piece of delicious cheese on top of a mouse trap. "It reminded me of another missing girl. Maybe it was because they went missing from the same place. I don't think they ever found the girl that went missing in 1980," Ted said, his heart beating faster. It wasn't racing, but it was thumping quick. It felt good to talk about what he'd done. "They'll never find that girl, or the one that's missing now."

Bob swayed nervously in his seat and said, "Why do you say that? Don't you have hope?"

Ted remained quiet while he thought about what to say next. "Do you want to go for a walk? I get restless legs. There's a trail out back."

"Oh, I don't know. My knees aren't too good for walking," Bob returned.

"Just for a little while. What do you say? It'll be good to get some blood pumping through your legs," Ted said, unable to contain the smile that seized his face. He stood from his chair. "Bring your coffee."

7

Robert had never been so scared. He thought, for sure, that Ted knew who he was. And he didn't want to go for a walk. Robert had had enough, and he could take what he'd learned back to the station. On the other hand, he still thought that Ted might not have figured him out yet. Maybe he did want to go for a walk. Old men do that. Hesitantly, Robert stood and followed Ted out the back door.

Outside in the sunshine, Robert realized how spread out the property was. It must be fifty acres or more. Looking over at Ted, he saw the same maniacal grin that he'd observed over two decades ago.

"Come on, Bob," Ted said, waving his free hand toward the tall grass. Now, from the backyard, he clearly saw the barn off to the left side of the house. It was eerie. There was no way to explain it, but the barn looked evil, like Ted. He watched as Ted walked down the beaten path.

Instinctively, Robert wanted to run. But for reasons unknown, he found himself stepping foot-over-foot down the small, cracked, cement stairs and toward the dirt trail leading into the field behind Ted's house.

The property was filled with large egg-shaped dirt mounds that jutted up from the ground. Most of them were covered with tall, thin grass, but the rise in the earth was still very noticeable.

"Maybe just for minute," Robert responded.

They walked in silence. Ted kept smiling and at one point, he even laughed.

About a hundred feet down the trail, Ted stopped in front of one of the mounds and pointed his index finger toward it. "You asked why I don't have hope. To be honest with you— about those missing kids—I know they'll never be found because I killed them." He was laughing again. "I mean I fucking killed them. That girl back in 1980 . . . I fucked her head after I cut it off . . . for three days. You know what it's like to stick your dick inside of a decapitated head?" His eyes met Robert. "Detective Grabske."

Robert dropped his coffee mug and spun away from Ted. He walked fast, joints aching, and then ran. His knees ached with each stride. He was grunting and huffing as he went, sweat dripping from his forehead. A searing pain shuttered through his hips, and he had to stop.

Something hit Robert in the side. He looked down and saw a large knife protruding from the right side of his body. Blood pumped out from around the metal blade and soaked his pants. Ted was walking toward him, still smiling.

Ted called out to him, "Just stop. I want to talk to you. Just listen to what I have to say, and I won't kill you . . . slow."

The pain was bad, but Robert continued to limp away from Ted. He wasn't going to escape this. Not this time. Coming out here had been a mistake.

He thought of Gina, sweet Gina.

8

"Is that your real name . . . Bob?" Ted asked, pulling the serrated knife from Bob's side. More blood erupted when the blade pulled free.

The old man shook his head, moaning in agonizing pain. "Robert. My name is Robert."

Ted cocked his head to the side and smiled. "Well, I guess you didn't necessarily lie then, did you?"

Robert started to fall, but before his knees hit the ground, Ted yanked him up by his arms. He dragged Robert down the dirt path, toward the house, and back in through the screen door.

In the kitchen, Ted sat Robert in his chair, filled up a fresh mug of coffee for him, then sat down and looked him square in the eye. "I really don't know why I didn't gut you like a deer and bury you. I got an extra hole out back. It was meant for someone else . . . the girl you were inquiring about. I just didn't get a chance to bury her there. Things went a little sideways."

Robert was hunkered over. But he must have been listening, because he tilted his head up, scowled and asked, "The girl from the papers? Jules Benton?"

"Is that her name?" Ted asked, sipping his coffee. "Those aren't the only scores I've taken. There have been a whole lot more. You saw the graves out back?"

Robert nodded, his eyebrows lifted, and he looked out the back door, which was still wide open. "All the hills?"

Ted's lips stretched wide, exposing his yellow teeth. "All of them. I like them blonde, Robert. I like them fit. It's nature, really. All animals kill other animals. I'm just enlightened enough to accept that. I enjoy killing the girls just like the lion enjoys killing the zebra and the cat enjoys killing the mouse. It's a cycle Robert . . . nothing more and nothing less. It's natural that you found me. You knew it was me all those years back, didn't you? Do you remember what you said to me . . . as you were leaving out the front door . . . you whispered, 'Did you kill those kids?', didn't you?"

Robert nodded his head again. "Yes, I did."

Ted watched Robert's face lose color but didn't know if it was from the loss of blood or the grim truth of the tale he told. "You need a glass of water, Robert?" Ted asked. He stood up and went to the sink.

9

When Robert saw that Ted's back was turned, he sprung from his chair and hobbled out the back door. He fell down the back stairs, but quickly stood and ran into the tall grass. The stab wound on his side throbbed, and his legs ached. Adrenaline was the only strength he possessed. The grass was damp, and he could feel the wetness soaking into his pants and shirt. Tripping over one of the graves, his face smacked the ground. A blinding white flash cut his vision.

He turned over and felt Ted's cold eyes. Pain stabbed at his knees and ankles. Pushing off the ground was useless, and he dropped to his back. The stab wound was kicking hard.

Robert felt like giving up. Ted was staring down at him.

"How did you know it was me?" Ted asked.

Robert scanned Ted from his worn-out boots, up to his filthy overalls and the neck of his sweat-stained white tee-shirt. Ted had no weapons now that Robert could see, but then again, he hadn't seen the knife either. "Your eyes," Robert finally answered. "Your eyes aren't human . . . they're empty."

Robert must have complimented him. Throughout the visit, he'd seen the maniacal smile, but now he was seeing appreciation. And suddenly, Robert felt that he wanted answers too. "How did you remember me? You even knew my name."

"I remember you from all those years back. I knew then that our business wasn't finished . . . it might be *now* though. A lot of things have changed lately. To be honest, I think my days might be numbered too. I can feel it coming . . . the end. So, here's to it." He saluted Robert.

Robert closed his eyes when Ted kneeled down beside him and pulled the knife from his back pocket. The grass tickled his face. Robert was afraid. Gina came through the darkness.

There was pain when Ted's callused hands clamped around Robert's neck. The knife blade was cold when it sliced into the thin skin of his throat.

Ted twisted Robert's head side to side.

There was an unpleasant snap, and then Robert saw Gina.

10

Ted looked down at the headless dead man lying in the grass. He'd actually liked the old man. And it was true what he'd said about having unfinished business. For many years, Ted knew this man would be back. On some level, they'd been searching for each other. It was a hunt and it represented something new.

And as Ted held Robert's bloody head in his hand, he knew that the end was coming.

Chapter 20
Richard's Plan

1

Richard Benton lay in bed, sleepless. Mary tossed and turned, moans escaping her mouth, but at least she was asleep. A few weeks earlier, he would have woken her up from this nightmare. Now, he wanted her to rest, even if it was a troubled rest. He rolled over onto his back and stared at the ceiling. Sleep never came to him that night, only the tick-tock of the clock ticking in his head. He had until Friday to deal with David. Could he do it?

In the morning, Richard got dressed, as usual, and had coffee with breakfast before leaving the house. Again, he called in sick, and his employer was happy to give him the day off. Before getting into his truck, he walked to the back of the garage and retrieved his shovel. It hung on the wall next to the hoe, rake, pick, and axe.

The sunlight that shone through the open garage door sent a glimmer down the blade of the axe and drew his attention to it.

Shovel in hand, he left the garage.

He set the shovel in the truck bed, climbed into the cab, and drove off.

He didn't enjoy lying to his wife, but in this case it was necessary. In his heart, he wanted to tell her of his plan to dispose of David. Intuitively, she would know he had something to do with David's disappearance and he wouldn't be able to hide it from her.

The highway was empty for the most part as he drove north toward his plot of land in northern Dodge County. It wasn't far, only forty miles and the scenery was nice. Just him, the road, his coffee, and his thoughts—it was calming. The last time he'd been up north was in November for deer hunting season. He'd shot a six-point buck and there was still venison meat stashed away in the basement freezer.

The plot was twelve acres of forest with a very small one bedroom cabin, tucked behind the pine trees near the front of the lot. It was simply a place to sleep during hunting season.

Richard parked his truck in the driveway, grabbed his shovel, marched a few hundred feet into the woods, and began digging. It was morbid and unpleasant digging a grave for a human being that he intended to kill in cold blood. Scratch that, he was going to kill a killer and somehow, someway, it would create balance. Killing David would not bring Jules back, but it would allow Richard to feel that justice had been served.

It took him just over three hours to dig the hole. When he finished, the grave was close to five feet deep. He climbed out and sat on the mound of loose dirt. The soil was moist and soon his pants were damp, and his butt itched. He stood up. Life stopped. Gritting his teeth, he tilted his head up to the sky. "What am I doing?" he screamed at the top of his lungs, knowing that no one could hear him but God. He fell to his knees and arched his back, closed his eyes, and clapped his hands together. "What do I do? Show me!"

Richard stayed there for over an hour. By the time he realized that he needed to get home, his legs were numb. With wobbly legs and a broken mind, he shuffled to his truck.

2

The sun had set significantly, casting a pink tone to the evening. The picturesque sky usually soothed Richard. Now, it could not exhaust his racing thoughts. The only image in his mind was David. He'd prayed for direction and received no answer.

The truck's engine stopped rumbling, and all was silent. His head pounded. He hadn't had any water since this morning, and he was dehydrated. The kitchen door swung open and fluorescent light illuminated the dark garage. Mary stood in the doorway with her hands resting on her hips. Although he couldn't see her face, he knew she was frowning.

"Where have you been? You're full of dirt. What's happening?" she demanded.

He didn't answer, nor did he stop to face her. He walked through the kitchen, down the hallway, and stopped in front of Jules' room. He twisted the knob and opened the door. The smell of Jules wafted into his nostrils, making him feel content for a short moment.

Mary followed him into the bedroom and halted, looking down at the floor. "Richard, you're tracking mud all over the floor. What has gotten into you?"

Finally, he looked up at her. As if in slow motion, their eyes met, and Mary took a seat at the foot of the bed. "Is she . . ."

"It was him . . . David."

"How do you . . ."

Richard reached down under the mattress and retrieved Jules' diary. He handed it to Mary.

"What is it?"

"It's her diary. She was pregnant. We had a grandchild . . ." He began to sob. "And he killed her."

"No, I don't believe you," she said, shaking her head while tears sprinted down her cheeks and spilled onto the pages of the journal. She quickly wiped her face.

"Most of it is in there," Richard said, drawing a deep breath. He needed to tell her, and he might as well do it now. "I skipped work the past few days . . . to follow David. He went out to the place where he did it . . . where he killed our daughter."

Mary silenced her sobbing. Her body shook as though she were going into a seizure.

"I followed him there. That piece of trash apologized to her grave . . . and I heard it all. He killed Jules because she was pregnant, Mary. Our little girl is dead because of that selfish puke." He continued explaining while digging his fingernails deep into his palms.

When Richard finished talking, Mary seemed composed. Through her sniffles she asked, "What about the police? Did they arrest him?"

Richard shook his head. There were no words for what needed to be said next.

Mary surprised him. "Good."

Richard's eyes went wide. "We're together on this?"

"And we don't even need to say anything . . . out loud. The less said the better. I know what needs to be done. But know this . . . I support you. Just make it back to me."

And with that, Richard nodded. He stood and left Mary in Jules' room. He knew his wife inside and out. Right now, she needed to be alone in this room.

"One last thing. He's going to turn himself in on Friday."

Mary wiped her eyes and said, "Then I guess you should hurry."

Richard looked down at his muddy pants. "I already have."

Chapter 21
Putting It Together

1

Detective Finley sat behind his cheap metal desk with his feet propped up and slurped down his lukewarm coffee, which had been sitting on his desk for an hour. The granulated sugar had separated and settled at the bottom, creating a sweet paste.

He opened the cream-colored folder resting in front of him with his large hands. Inside was a picture of Jules Benton to go with his case file. He'd talked to Penny Sloan, Mark Tisdale, and a few other kids that associated with Jules. Also, he'd talked to David Miller in the presence of his father. David answered everything smoothly. Said that he'd dropped Jules off at home a little after midnight, then drove home. His parents corroborated his story. *The Benton's said she never came home.* Finley was not going to rule out foul play. Being a police officer in Los Angeles had taught him never to overlook anything. The answer sometimes rested outside the box. Jules may very well have been abducted and murdered, used in a sick sex act, and burned to ashes—he'd seen it before. On a lighter note, maybe she had an older, secret lover. She may have been using David as a cover for her relationship with this older man. The possibilities were endless, and each time Finley came up with a new scenario he would write it down in his yellow notepad. As he investigated and found that his theories didn't hash out, he would scratch a single line through each idea and move on to the next. Intuition, like a theory, was not to be ignored, and Finley liked David as the culprit. In his mind, David was the prime suspect and even with an alibi, he was not crossed off the list. Sure, he seemed like a nice enough kid. But so did Ted Bundy and Jeffery Dahmer. Plus, he didn't even know if Jules Benton was dead or not. Added to which, David couldn't explain the wounds that were inflicted to his hands. There were scabs and blisters peppered across both of his palms. They looked like the kind of wounds that incurred when one shovels without gloves. He had asked, prodded and pried for an answer from David but in the end, he'd said nothing, and his parents assured him that he didn't need to say anything more.

He looked through the Benton file again. He wanted to approach David Miller alone, but how? Without solid evidence there was only speculation and that never flew in court. There had to be something material.

Going to David Miller's house was sounding like an increasingly good idea. Maybe he could catch him before school, get him away from his parents and see what he could find out. It would allow him to get out of the office for a while.

And right now, that sounded like a great idea.

Chapter 22
The Drive

1

On Thursday morning, David woke up from a pleasant dream. In it, everything was normal, the same as it was a month ago—peaceful and ordinary. Then David's eyes shot open to the realization that he was a monster. He wanted to skip school today and spend time with his parents. He wouldn't have much time with them in the near future.

They couldn't know what he'd done just yet.

Maybe he could admit what he'd done to them, and they would understand?

His father would probably tell him to be quiet, shut his mouth, and would call his lawyer. The lawyer would instruct him on what to say. But in truth, he didn't want to be a monster anymore. He wanted to confess the awful crime that he'd committed, and he wanted to serve his punishment, so that he could possibly salvage some kind of a life.

He wanted to make things right, for Jules' sake.

Penny had stopped by last night to ask if he knew where Jules was. He had remained silent for a long time while Penny waited with her arms crossed on his porch. "Go home," he'd told her. In that moment, he'd found that he could no longer lie—there was only truth or silence.

"I know you had something to do with this," she'd said.

After she had said that, his first thought was to kill her and he had looked around the neighborhood to see if anyone was watching. He could have rushed her, choked the life out of her, but for what?

He had turned his back on her and gone inside. Killing one person was bad enough. It was damning.

2

Eggs and bacon with a side of toast sat on the table in front of David. He drank his coffee and stared at his food. In the last week, he'd lost eight pounds. He couldn't eat. He didn't want to either. The scary part was that he couldn't. Even when he washed it down with water or orange juice, he would gag it back up.

He wished that he could go back in time.

He dropped his fork onto his plate and spoke to himself, "I would be better off dead."

The house was empty. His parents had both left for work at six-thirty.

In the bathroom, he took his brown leather belt and wrapped it around the shower rod. He hoped that it was strong enough. The rod was metal, and it was plastered into the dry wall and secured with a bracket and cover.

David twisted the belt around the rod, stuck his head inside of the belt loop and looked down at his bare feet. Though about to commit suicide, the only thought trapped inside his head was that his toenails needed to be clipped. He bent his knees and let the belt sink into the soft flesh of his throat. He could feel the blood shutting off from his head and immediately he became dizzy. When he opened his mouth to breathe, he grasped nothing, no air. He began to shake, and bright colors exploded before his eyes, like green clouds expanding behind his eyelids.

His mouth opened and he tried to say, "Mom."

And then he stood up. He was too cowardly to do it. He couldn't go through with this. For the first time since the crime, he thought that he'd be doing the right thing. If his mother were to walk into the bathroom that evening after coming home from a hard day at work and see him hanging there, he didn't think that she could go on. So, he removed the belt from around his neck and got dressed for school.

Turning himself in was the right thing to do.

There were light pink marks across his throat. They weren't extreme. They would fade away in a matter of hours. He hadn't allowed himself to hang for very long, a few seconds at most. Not long enough to twist and kill his skin cells. His throat was a little sore, but that was all. He brushed his teeth and rinsed with mouthwash.

He grabbed his car keys, tossed them in the air, caught them, twisted the doorknob and left the house.

3

The sun shone brightly in the blue sky behind a few scattered clouds. The weather was perfect. Richard had the windows of his truck rolled down and the breeze cooled his hot skin. He was close now, driving down David's street. The Miller house was only a few more houses down and on the right. His eyes felt itchy and dry even though they were watering up.

Richard saw David lock the front door to the house and walk to his car. His nerves sped up and so did his truck. Richard came to a halt in front of the driveway. David looked at him and frowned.

Richard parked in front of the mailbox, got out and walked toward David. "Hey David, you got a minute?"

David didn't answer. Richard found himself wondering if David knew that *he knew*. He hoped that David would not see the axe that he'd placed in the bed of his truck, next to the shovel. "I got a minute. What can I do for you, Mr. Benton?"

"I was just thinking about Jules. I guess I was thinking about how I hadn't been real close with her for the past few years. You kids go on to high school and *we* become the bad guys," Richard said while twiddling his thumbs over each other in circular motions.

"We don't think you're the bad guys, Mr. Benton. We just keep wanting to do things you won't let us. It's more like a conflict of interest," David said with a quick grin.

Richard forced a smile. All he could think about was how nice it would feel to take David's head apart with the axe. The urge to kill was boiling inside of him. Although his nerves were nearly shot, he held his composure—for Jules' sake. "I really miss my daughter, David. I was hoping that maybe I could buy you some breakfast and we could just talk . . . about Jules."

David stepped back and looked to his neighbor's house. There was a short old man trudging down the walkway toward his mailbox. He waved and David waved back. "What do you want to talk about?"

"Well, like I said, I haven't had a chance to know Jules that well over the past few years. You could tell me what kind of things she likes and where she likes to go . . . things like that?"

David seemed to ease up and he said, "I have school."

Richard smiled wide and shrugged his shoulders. "I could probably vouch for you if you were to miss a few classes. I know the principal. It would only be for a few hours . . . .if that."

"Well, I guess it wouldn't hurt. I wouldn't be missing much anyway . . . and I don't really feel like going to school. I just can't concentrate." He started to walk back toward his car. "Where should I meet you?"

Richard fumbled for words and after a moment he said, "Why don't you hop in my truck?"

David stopped. They stared at each other for a few silent seconds. David bounced his keys in his wounded hand a few times and stuffed them into his pocket. "I guess that'd work." He trotted toward Richard.

Hard as it was, Richard wrapped his arms around David and squeezed him affectionately. "Thanks. I really need this." He couldn't stop staring at David's torn hands.

"No problem, Mr. Benton."

"Call me Rich."

"Okay . . . Rich."

They jumped into Richard's truck and David's neighbor waved as they drove away.

4

David and Richard made small talk while they drove toward the edge of town. Once Richard was past town limits, they both became quiet.

David wondered where they were going. Mr. Benton said that he wanted to talk, buy him breakfast or coffee. Now they were leaving town and Richard looked focused.

"Is everything all right, Rich?" he asked.

With obvious sarcasm, Richard replied, "Well, Jules is missing, and my life is falling apart without her, but besides that . . . I guess everything is peachy."

David's nerves were rattled. He suddenly wondered, as he had earlier, if Richard knew something. How could he have known anything? Maybe that cop figured it out and spilled the beans. The detective probably didn't have any material evidence, but he was letting Mr. Benton know that *he* was the prime suspect.

That had to be it.

"Is everything all right?" David asked again. "Didn't you just ask me that?"

David grabbed hold of the door handle and wrapped his fingers around it. Just in case. He had a frightful feeling that he may need to bail out of the truck. Richard was lowering his hand below his door handle and seemed to be fiddling with something under the seat.

David wiped sweat from his forehead. With a shaky voice he asked, "Can you stop the car?"

Richard snapped his head toward David. Now he was sure that Richard knew. The intensity in his eyes told all. His face was bright red, and he was gritting his teeth. Everything around David slowed to a crawl, as if the truck had stopped moving. Richard was staring at him.

David pulled on the door handle. Then he felt pressure on the back of his head and there was a rush of pain. The top of his head was hot and throbbing. He could barely hear anything. He spun around to face Richard.

There was a large silver hammer in his left hand. And he was swinging it down on David for the second time. It hit David in the face and his front teeth broke and tore from his gums. The pain struck, sudden and intense. The broken edges of his front teeth dug into his bottom lip and the blood felt cold as it ran down his chin. He became nauseated from the overwhelming pain. Somehow, he pulled the door handle and shoved it open.

David toppled out of the car.

Ground . . . sky . . . ground . . . sky . . . he rolled over and over and then felt a heavy kick to his stomach. He saw white.

5

Richard slammed on the brakes and jumped out of the truck. He ran back about fifty feet toward David, searching the area for anyone watching but he saw nothing. He stuck his hands underneath David's armpits and dragged him back to the truck.

David's body thumped down—hard—on the road in front of the truck bed. Richard pulled the latch, picked David up, and shoved him toward the back next to the shovel and axe. He hoped that David would remain unconscious for at least fifteen more minutes. That would be enough time for Richard to take him to his land up north.

Richard closed up the truck bed, hurried over to the driver's side, jumped in and sped off, leaving a short black line of rubber on the asphalt.

Chapter 23
Mary's Ultimatum

1

Detective Finley pulled into the Miller's driveway at a little past seven o'clock and parked behind David's car. Content that he'd caught David before school, Finley walked to the front door and rang the bell.

He waited for thirty seconds and rang it again.

Nothing.

Turning to the house next door, Finley saw an elderly man watching him from an open garage. He was sitting in an aluminum lawn chair with checkered straps. A Pabst Blue Ribbon swayed in his left hand.

"There ain't no one home over there!" the man shouted.

Finley decided to humor himself. He walked across the Miller's lawn and made his introduction. "I'm Detective Finley." He stuck out his hand.

The elderly man set his beer can down on the cement driveway and took Finley's hand.

"What were you just saying?" Finley asked.

"I said there ain't no one home over at the Miller place."

"Oh, I just figured . . . since the car was in the driveway . . ." Finley continued. He was probably wasting his time again, but you never knew.

"Usually, the kid takes that car, but today some older fellow picked him up. By the way, I'm Jim. Jim Levasseur. When you get to be my age you develop a knack for eavesdropping on your neighbors. My wife likes to sit in her reclining chair and watch the damn television. I like to watch the neighborhood."

Finley found Jim entertaining but if he stuck around too long, the poor guy would end up talking his afternoon away. "Did you say an older fellow picked him up?"

"Yeah, had a blue truck . . . a Ford. I'm a Chevy man myself, but at least it's American." Finley laughed.

"The older gentleman had dark hair, probably in his late forties," Jim said while reaching down and grabbing his Pabst. *Richard Benton. It had to be Richard.*

"They seem like they were getting along?" Finley asked.

"Wasn't anything too strange . . . other than David should have been going to school. Maybe that guy was taking him there, I don't know."

"Thanks, Jim. Take it slow with those barley pops."

"I never drank much until now. I'm old and I don't have to worry about it killing me . . . I'm old."

Finley left and there was urgency in his step as his intuitive mind spun with dark ideas. He needed to get over to the Benton's house. He had a strong feeling that Richard might know something. How could he not? The circumstantial evidence against David was quite compelling and Finley did not want a distraught father taking the law into his own hands.

2

Mary was spread out on the living room couch watching daytime television when Detective Finley knocked at the front door. She immediately got up and answered.

Finley had a nice face, and his constant inquisition made him mysterious. Mary was growing a little bit of a crush.

Not that she would act on it, but it was there. Richard was the love of her life.

How could she be thinking girlish thoughts while her husband was out killing that boy?

"Hi Mary," Finley said. "Is Richard home?"

"No. He's at work."

"He's not. I called the bottling factory and they said he hadn't been to work in a couple of days." Mary's skin went cold as ice.

What was the detective getting at? Was he on to the plan?

"That's news to me, Detective," Mary said while processing the hard look on his face.

"Do you mind if I come in for a moment?"

Mary stepped aside and he entered, looking around the living room. She directed him to a chair. "I have a pot of coffee on, would you care for a cup?"

"Sure, that would be kind of you."

Finley took a seat on the chair across from the couch, near the picture window. He leaned forward and propped his chin up on his knuckles.

"What can I help you with?" Mary called out from the kitchen.

"I just wanted to ask you a few questions," he said.

Mary carried two mugs of coffee into the living room. "Oh, did you want sugar and cream?" she asked.

3

Finley did want sugar and cream, but he needed answers right now and he needed them quick. "No, I like it black," he lied.

"Well, what can I help you with then?" she asked, returning to the couch.

"Your husband was seen picking up David Miller earlier this morning. Do you know where they went?"

Mary lifted the mug to her lips and sipped. When she lowered the mug, it began to tremble, and she steadied it with her free hand.

"Is something wrong, Mary?"

"N . . . no, huh, uh. Why would anything be wrong?"

Undoubtedly, she was nervous. She had to know something.

"I'm just going to say this for the sake of saying it . . . if Richard is planning to do something—something that should be handled by the authorities—then you have an obligation to tell me what you know."

Her face turned red. She set her mug down on the table too hard, and a few droplets of coffee jumped out and landed on the wooden surface. "What are you getting at?"

"When I showed up here, you didn't ask me if I had any news about Jules. You didn't ask for an update . . . and quite frankly, we both know that something is going on here, *something* that could potentially get *someone* in a lot of trouble. That's not like you at all. You know something."

Gritting her teeth, Mary looked like she was going to snap. "My husband is a good man, and he does the right thing. I only wish I had the strength to be more like him. I don't know what you're implying, but maybe it would be better if you left."

Finley set his coffee down and stood up. "I apologize. Just know that I want what's best for you and your husband. If he does something stupid right now, he's going to end up in jail." "Get out," Mary whispered. She was crying now.

Finley was sure that something was not right. And he was determined to find out what was happening. It might take him a little time, but it didn't take Sherlock Holmes to realize that Mary was hiding something.

"You have property up in North Dodge County, is that correct?" Finley asked as he twisted the doorknob.

At first, he was genuinely concerned by how pale she suddenly appeared. Hands at her side, slightly trembling, she stood silent.

That's it!

Richard was taking David to the property up north and the possibilities of what he might be planning to do with him were not positive. He could be wrong, but he couldn't take the chance. Finley would call the Dodge County sheriff's department and ask them to check out the property.

"Wait," she said, turning toward the hallway. Her face was ghostly pale, and she was perspiring. With a sickly face like that, Finley knew she was drowning in a lie. "In Jules' room, there's a journal."

Finley followed her down the hallway and into a bedroom. He was glad that she had come to her senses, even though she might be incriminating herself.

He wanted to help the Benton family. They were good people going through a tough time. Also, he might find evidence incriminating David Miller. If he could get to the boy before Richard did anything, everything might be all right.

In the bedroom, Mary lifted the mattress and pulled out a diary. She handed it to Finley and said, "I'll go get your

coffee and then I'll tell you everything."

The diary felt heavy in Finley's hands.

He sat down on the bed and opened it to the first page.

4

Mary grabbed their mugs from the living room and went into the kitchen. She was trembling. If she told Finley what she knew then Richard would certainly go to prison for the rest of his life. Like a dagger through her chest, the thought of living without Richard tore into her. Never in his life would he forgive her for this. She would not only lose her precious daughter, but she would also lose her husband. Everything that she loved in this world would be taken from her.

Looking at the coffee in the mug, a thought came to her. It was the darkest thought she'd ever conjured—a vision of dumping poison into the detective's mug and serving it to him. No. She couldn't. For one, she had no poison, besides bleach, and he would certainly smell that from a mile away, let alone drink it. Second, she wasn't a murderer. However, her life had changed in the blink of an eye—thrice—in the last few weeks. First: when her daughter had gone missing. Second: when she discovered that her daughter was dead. Third: when she had given her husband permission to kill the boy who had murdered their daughter. Things had become complicated. She wasn't the person she'd thought she was, and now she was capable of things she never imagined. She didn't recognize herself. The stakes were higher. She would do anything for her family, and therefore she thought that she could.

Could what? She wasn't going to go into Jules' bedroom and just kill a police officer. She had no gun and if she went in with a knife, Finley would easily take her down. She could go to prison too. Another vision forced its way into her head while she refreshed the mugs with coffee.

This one she acted on.

Mary put the coffee inside the microwave and set the timer for three minutes. Way too long for a cup of coffee.

5

Mary entered Jules' room and walked toward Finley as he flipped through Jules' diary. His neck slowly tilted up to face her, eyes squinted. Immediately frowning, he set the diary down on the bed and held his hand out to her. Mary thought he looked nervous.

Extending her shaky hand out to him, he met the mug with splayed fingers. She let her hand unravel from around the mug. She gave it a little push when his hand met hers just below her fingers. The mug fell from both their hands. Finley's hand followed the mug down to his chest where he tried to grab it. It was too late.

"Damn it! That's ho . . ." he started to say, then cried out in agony as the scalding hot coffee spilled onto his gray slacks around his groin area.

When he jumped up from the bed, she withdrew the Cuisinart butcher knife from her back pocket and plunged it upward into Finley's neck just below his jaw line. It felt like stabbing into a watermelon.

Finley's attention left his groin and quickly shot to his neck. He seemed to be inspecting the wound, tapping his fingers around the outside of the blade where his flesh had been penetrated. Blood was spurting from his throat in thick currents. He looked at her and tried to speak, but all he could manage to do was gargle. Thick blood mixed with bubbles and saliva seeped from between his lips and made his mouth look clown-like. He fumbled and fell to his knees. He yanked the knife free. An amazing explosion of crimson blood erupted when the silver blade slid from his neck.

Mary watched—amazed, but not horrified—as Finley crawled toward her. His hand drew back to his belt.

Mary's eyes went wide when she heard the hammer of Finley's gun click into action.

A shot rang out.

Chapter 24
Anxious Ted

1

Taking the old man, Robert, as a score wasn't enough to quench Ted's murderous appetite. Neither was the blonde score that he'd only partially taken, weeks earlier. He needed to hunt, and for the first time, patience was something he was willing to overlook. After taking a few moments to catch his breath—burying Robert had spent a bit of his energy—he went back into the house.

Burning Robert's corpse earlier had set fire to Ted's desire for murder. He wanted the journey, the stalk, the fight, the kill . . . the ritual. He would hop a few towns over and look for a fresh score. It was morning, but maybe he would get lucky.

As Ted walked to the barn, he noticed scattered driblets of blood soaked into the dirt. He kicked it around with his boots and continued on his way.

He had a sinking feeling in his stomach as he drove the van out of the barn. Normally, he would take this as a warning, but the urge to find a score was too great. He would be fine if he just left town and found a vulnerable score, maybe a child?

As he drove away from his property, relief hit when the excitement of anticipation encouraged him. Thoughts of killing surged through his mind. He grasped the steering wheel tight and remembered the girl, not the one he'd taken over two decades ago, but the one he'd taken at The Garden.

His property disappeared slowly in the rearview mirror and then he was on County Trunk A, headed toward Juneau; a town just over thirty miles north.

Chapter 25
Going Through With It

1

The familiar sound of twigs, leaves, and gravel crunched beneath the tires of Richard Benton's truck. He felt no connection with the *thing* lying unconscious in the truck bed. To Richard, David was a rabid dog that needed to be put down.

After parking next to the cabin, he turned his head toward the truck bed. It swayed side to side as though a log were rolling back and forth. Richard's heart raced when he saw David climbing out. His arms were draped over the wheel well and he was trying to lift himself over the edge. The sight was comical. Even if David were able to get out, he was in no shape to run. He'd probably broken his legs and maybe a few ribs when he jumped out of the truck earlier—who knew what else.

Richard got out and walked around to the bed. "You planning on going somewhere?" He grabbed David's arms and yanked them forward with all of his strength. David flopped over the edge and twirled once before landing on top of his head and curling into a ball near the rear tire. He moaned and howled.

Richard dragged David across the driveway and into the woods. Richard's muscles ached and strained from the weight, and David's legs kicked from side to side, which, ironically, helped Richard's momentum as he dragged him toward his own grave.

About a hundred feet into the woods, Richard dropped David next to the hole he'd dug. David's face went ashen with terror. He could tell that David didn't want to die.

Good.

Neither did Jules.

Any second thoughts or feelings of guilt that Richard anticipated were absent. Stomping on David's head behind the ear was liberating. When David groaned, Richard's blood boiled with rage. His back teeth grated, and he had to force himself to stop before he broke them.

Hurting David felt great. Richard had never been more alive in his life.

Inhibitions ceased.

Watching David pull himself away from the hole was comical and laughter was on the tip of his tongue. The steel toes of his boots probably hurt immensely when he kicked David with them, which inspired him to kick David in the face three more times.

After the third kick, David rolled over onto his back and his eyelids slowly drooped.

Richard went back to his truck and gathered his tools. David was twitching, but probably couldn't think clearly enough to escape, nor did he have the physical means to get away. Richard whistled while he walked through the forest toward his Ford.

A sense of ultimate power surged through him when he picked up the heavy axe. He shifted the worn wooden handle from his right hand to his left, acknowledging the weight. He watched the shimmer of reflective light run down the sharp edge of the blade and twinkle near the top. His face was burning, and he craved the kill. His lips slowly stretched across his face into an insane smile.

David had managed to crawl twenty feet away.

Richard stopped walking and held the axe with both hands. His right hand squeezed the wooden handle just below the blade while his left grasped the handle about six inches from the bottom. Breath came in deep waves. His chest pumped in and out. Blood was blasting through his veins, and he was gritting his teeth again.

In a storm of rage, Richard sprinted forward. David's head dipped down as if bracing for the chop.

The blade crashed down onto David's right leg and sunk deep into his flesh. Richard's wrist shook when the blade hit bone. And he was certain that he'd broken David's leg.

David howled, gutturally, while Richard withdrew the axe and wielded it down again, almost in the same spot. This time, David's leg rolled over to the side and

Richard could see the meat spilling out where he'd severed it. Blood gushed in thick torrents.

When Richard raised the axe again, blood sprayed across his chest and face. The warm crimson fluid made him feel amazingly powerful. The axe hammered down and slammed into David's back with a loud thump. He heard the remaining air expel from David's lungs.

Richard chopped David again, unable to stop.

Chapter 26
Mary's Choice

1

Mary felt wobbly. The blast from Finley's gun hit the side of her face. Her hand was soaked with blood and only shreds of flesh remained on the right side of her head where her ear used to be. It stung. Blood made Mary nauseous. And there was blood everywhere.

Mary had drenched her daughter's room with the blood of an innocent cop who only wanted to help find her. A murderer, that's what she was now. She had killed a cop, and she couldn't see herself getting out of this one. The neighbors had probably heard the shot ring out and they had probably called 911. There might be more cops on their way as she stood, mortified, over the bloodied body of Detective Finley. She needed Richard. Mentally he was stronger than her, he always had been. Together they could fix this, but she needed him right now, and he wasn't there.

He was out in the woods killing David.

Blood pouring down the side of her face and onto her brand new, white, button-down shirt, Mary hustled through the kitchen and grabbed the keys.

Slow throbs bounced back and forth from the left side of her head to the right. There was a ringing sensation, which made her dizzy. She stumbled through the garage until she found the side of her Jeep and felt her way to the doorhandle.

Lofting herself inside the driver's seat, she drew deep breaths and forced herself to settle down. If she could just find Richard, they could figure everything out.

Together.

With a twitchy hand, she forced the key into the ignition and the rumble of her Jeep's engine sprung to life.

Her foot eased on the gas, then quickly slammed on the brakes.

She almost crashed through the closed garage door.

Her right hand rose to the sun visor where the small black garage door opener was clipped. She pushed the white button in the middle and the screech of the garage door faintly pierced her mutilated ear. The sunlight stabbed at her hazy eyes causing her to squint, then she left the house.

Her forehead was almost touching the windshield. Her vision was far from clear right now and she not only felt nauseated, but she also felt faint.

The steering wheel was locked. She looked in the rearview mirror and realized that she'd driven into the middle of the street, then across it. Her back tire was snubbed up against the curb. It occurred to her that she should not be behind the wheel of an automobile. Like the little bottles of pain medication read: "may impair your driving." *The same went for flesh wounds*, she thought.

Blood was caked on the driver-side window and starting to dry. If she were to drive past a cop right now, she would surely be pulled over. That couldn't happen. If she could just get out to their property without being spotted, she could find Richard and he would tell her what to do. The only reason she'd killed that detective was to save her family. Family came first. Even before the law. Hopefully, Finley was dead, and no one had heard the gunshot. When she left the house, she didn't notice anything out of place about the neighborhood. No one was standing in the yard gaping at her. No judgmental fingers aimed at her as she thought there may have been. Just empty green lawns and a few picket fences.

Relief washed over her when she saw the sign reading County Trunk A. That meant she was on the right track and headed toward their property. It was forty miles of rural terrain.

Chapter 27
Ted's Drive

1

Ted drove slowly down the empty back road, taking in the bright sunny morning.
Everything would be fine.

His eagerness to kill was subsiding, still strong, but it wasn't controlling his thoughts anymore. Earlier, he wasn't able to control his urges. He would have killed the first person to cross his path. And that was only ten minutes ago.

Now, he would go north and find a little town, maybe scout around outside of a grocery store and wait for a nice score. A young one. They were easier and quicker to catch. He could buy some candy or chips and lure one into his van. He could take *it* back to his property and play with *it*.

That was what he'd been missing.

He hadn't been able to play with his last few scores, and it was making him edgy. The old man, the girl; neither had fulfilled him. And the blonde—out at The Garden—wasn't enough. She hadn't completed the full act. He needed the rush that came with stalking a score and the thrill of being vulnerable for a few short seconds before he had the score incapacitated and out of sight. That was what he lived for.

County Trunk A would take him where he wanted to go. As long as he got himself forty or fifty miles away from Watertown, he could feel at ease. There probably wasn't much noise about the missing girl in the northwestern towns like Viroqua or La Farge. It may have been a page three story in the local newspaper, but that was all.

Ted eagerly licked his lips as he drove through the vast acreage of forest and green fields.

Chapter 28
Colliding

1

Richard held David's head in his hand, fascinated by the blood draining onto the ground from the torn veins and arteries. The throat looked like a snapped twig covered in blood. His fingers were tangled in the dark brown hair of David's scalp. He held the head high, at eye level. The ease with which he had desecrated this human being was unnerving. Richard was changed now. He wondered what else he was capable of doing.

David's black pupils seemed to be staring directly into Richard's soul. He asked himself what David had been thinking when he'd taken Jules. If he had felt this same rush of power, the overwhelming surge of adrenaline that came with killing—the taking of a human life.

Then he threw David's head into the oval-shaped hole with the rest of the body parts.

David's legs had come off first. Richard had enjoyed watching David's attempt to crawl away while his amputated legs remained behind. After a few feet, he'd stopped and whimpered like a starving dog.

This went on for at least five minutes. David hadn't died until his head came off. After the previous chop that landed in his back, Richard could sense that his life was draining quickly, but when he slammed the metal axe blade into David's neck—that's when he stopped moving. The world around Richard seemed to stop too. David's torso and arms simply slumped flat against the ground, and he died. That didn't keep Richard from chopping into him again. He must have slammed the axe into David forty times or more. Richard wanted David's body to be the way his soul felt—apart.

He had kicked the remaining limbs into the hole like trash except for the head, which he wanted to inspect. To hold it and know that he'd received the justice he sought after, for Jules.

Filling in the hole with dirt went quick, just over a half an hour. He stood over the grave and nodded. The feelings of satisfaction that he anticipated did not come to him, as he assumed they would. And for one quick moment, he asked himself if there was a possibility that David wasn't the man who'd killed Jules.

He'd confessed to the murder, had gone out to the grave where he'd buried her and asked for forgiveness.

Richard hocked a wad of phlegm onto David's grave and went back to his truck. The need to get home and be with Mary suddenly grew fierce. He needed to hear and believe that everything was going to be all right. He needed to be comforted.

He started the engine and drove back down the dirt path toward the road. His work clothes were covered in blood, and he needed to burn them, or at least make them disappear.

The path from the cabin was rocky. He'd meant to dig up the rocks last summer but hadn't gotten around to it. He'd chalked it up as *not important* if he recalled correctly.

Unable to fully concentrate on the dirt path, he swerved to the right, then quickly cranked the wheel to the left when he saw the ditch ahead of him, at the base of the road.

The front of Richard's truck dipped down and he watched it rise with mounting horror. Whizzing as opposed to rumbling, the engine sputtered and the shocks bounced when the wheels hit solid ground. The truck shook violently and there was a loud crunch. He could feel the muffler smash as it hit the ground.

He wondered if he should stop and inspect the damage. He turned the engine off and jumped out of the truck.

Lowering himself to the ground, his frustration mounted when he saw the muffler and exhaust pipe bent all to hell and he knew that the drive home was now going to be a messy one.

Panic.

The engine rumbled loudly as he drove out of the driveway. He needed to get home before the truck stopped running or the muffler fell off. Things were going wrong and for the first time—in a long time—he felt God's vengeful eye frowning upon him. He'd done bad things, broken the commandments and now he was going to feel the wrath. He felt punishment sink into his blood and suddenly the hair on his forearms stood up high from his tough skin.

Leaving black rubber marks on the pavement when his tires hit the highway, Richard sped off.

2

Mary had already traveled twenty-five of the forty miles to the cabin. There had been no traffic up until a few minutes ago. A beat-up white van had been driving too slow in front of her. Dizzy and out of breath from the loss of blood and the shock of her morning, she'd attempted to pass the van. She didn't drive ahead fast enough, and she pulled in too quickly. If the driver hadn't slammed on his brakes, they would have crashed. It was a close call. And even though Mary had much bigger problems to worry about, she sped ahead of the van feeling guilty for almost running him off the road. Road rage could get pretty ugly. What if the driver had caught up to her and given her a hard time?

The day was getting very messy.

She needed to be with Richard.

Her thoughts were clouded with dark matters. How had Richard done with David? Did he chicken out? And now, was the only mess they needed to clean up the one she'd left back at the house? Another vision draped her mind. This time she envisioned police cars surrounding her home. A stretcher with a white sheet draped over the corpse being extracted by two EMT's.

Things were bad, and Mary knew they would get worse.

Looking down at the speedometer, she realized that she was driving almost ninety miles an hour. She slowed down, looked in the rearview mirror and searched for any signs of the white van. When she had gotten close to hitting him, he'd looked over at her. There was no shocked expression upon his face, which struck her as odd. She was running him off the road and he was looking at her as though he recognized her, maybe trying to figure out where he knew her from. He looked older, his face was tan and weathered, but there was something fit about him, probably a farmer.

Ten more miles.

If she could make it that far, she could be with Richard. Maybe they could stay the night in the cabin, figure everything out, then deal with it tomorrow.

3

Ted's hands were steady on the steering wheel. Anger was something he had control over, and this time was no different. That woman in the Jeep Cherokee had almost run him off the road a few miles back and the only worry he had was that if she crashed into him, he wouldn't be able to get out of town and find a fresh score.

He needed a score.

Thank God he'd slammed on the brakes or else he'd be stuck a few miles back, stranded, waiting for the police. And he really didn't want to deal with them right now.

The woman in the car looked familiar. Almost like an older version of the score he'd assisted with. *No, couldn't be*. That would be too much of a coincidence. Her hair was blonde, her eyes blue, and there was something about the shape of her jaw. The way it came down to a defined slant. He couldn't shake the thought. *What were the odds that it was her mother?* Ted wondered.

Ted shrugged his shoulders as he drew a mental image of the woman. Was she bleeding? Now that he recalled, the side of her face was red, and the window too. Either that or she had spilled something, because the whole side of her body seemed to be soaked in dark red, or black. Maybe she was injured. That would explain why she was driving erratically.

Strange.

The last few days had been very strange. Things felt like they were coming to an end. The girl, the old man, all of it seemed to be leading toward some kind of conclusion. These were a series of events that seemed out of balance. Faith wasn't Ted's strong suit, but he couldn't help but feel that something bigger than himself, and everyone else, was causing *things* to happen on a much larger scale.

He started laughing and his eyes turned upward to the sky. "If you're planning on punishing me now, you're just a little late." And he continued to laugh out loud, shaking his head.

4

Richard had only traveled four miles. At first, the truck slowed down and his top speed had dropped to just over forty-five. Punching his foot on the gas pedal wasn't helping and the truck started to jerk violently. The muffler coughed up a black cloud of smoke. He realized that the exhaust pipes were pinched, and his truck wasn't going to make it home. And he needed to get home quick.

He pulled off to the shoulder and let the truck idle. And then it stopped. The axe and shovel were still back at the property, which was a good thing. If a cop came to assist him and found the bloody axe and dirty shovel, he might become suspicious.

It wasn't too often that blood-soaked grown men were spotted walking down the highway late in the morning, on a Thursday. This was the predicament that he was in, and he would have to figure a way out of it. He'd come too far to cash in now. If a sheriff or officer pulled over, he would just say that he'd hit a deer, dragged it to his truck and buried it back at his property. That sounded logical, especially out here in the back country of Wisconsin. That kind of thing happened all the time; except the part about burying the deer. Normally, one would either leave the deer on the side of the road or take it to a butcher.

What about his truck? Why weren't there any dings? "Well officer, I just kind of clipped him, then I ran into a ditch. If you take a look at my truck, you'll see that the muffler and exhaust are all shot to hell from pulling in and out of the ditch." That excuse made sense, he thought.

Time wasn't slowing down, so Richard started walking and hoped for the best. There was a hill coming up in less than a mile and Richard could already see the highway curving upward. He leaned forward and quickened his pace.

5

Mary slapped the back of her head in an attempt to stay awake. She was exhausted and felt like passing out. Even though she was wound up from the insanity of the day's events, she was fatigued.

Probably fair to assume that the loss of blood was a factor too.

At least she hadn't run into the cops.

The centerline disappeared underneath the Jeep. She was swerving again. She jerked the steering wheel and the Jeep abruptly swung right.

After slapping herself in the face, she straightened the car.

She was coming up on a hill. Best to be careful. She didn't want to hit anything on the other side. Eyelids drooping again, Mary drove over the hill, and she saw *him*.

Richard?

No.

Why would he be walking along the highway?

She hit the brakes.

The Jeep slid sideways and halted half-on and half-off the shoulder of the highway. She rolled down her window. He was covered in blood.

"What are you doing?" he asked, making his way to her side of the Jeep. "What happened to you?"

Shaking her head she said, "I don't want to talk about it. Maybe you should drive?" She realized that her speech had slurred. The reality of the situation was that she needed medical attention, and she needed it quick. It looked to her like Richard also needed help. His clothes and face were covered in blood. That would be a riot; entering Watertown Memorial Hospital covered in blood. She could walk up to Ruth Wilson, her friend from high school and nurse-in-charge of the emergency room, and say, "Hey Ruth. Rich and I just killed a seventeen-year-old boy and a cop. The cop shot me and the boy . . . well . . . we haven't exactly gotten to that yet . . . you got a spare gurney?" Mary was laughing out loud. Richard cocked his head and frowned at her.

A low rumble drifted through the morning air and stapled itself into Mary's ears.

The van that Mary had nearly crashed into slammed into Richard. His face smacked against the highway, and he slid down the center lane, leaving a wet red-brown trail behind him.

Before she could scream, she felt a growl in the pit of her stomach and her knees collapsed forward into her chest.

6

Richard forced his eyes open. The sun scorched them with brightness. There was a pounding sensation at the base of his neck that quickly throbbed forward and encompassed the entirety of his head. He felt something floating at the bottom of his tongue and he spit out a handful of blood-soaked teeth.

With all of his might, Richard tried to sit up. He couldn't. His brain was telling his legs to move, but there was no movement.

His arms: Nothing. His fingers: Nothing.

The only thing he felt was the pain in his head and that was far from any kind of relief.

To the side of the road, he saw a giant mass of twisted white metal. *Maybe a van?* The front end was smashed into what was left of Mary's Jeep, which looked like a crushed soda can.

Richard used his peripheral vision to see that Mary was cut in half and draped over the side of the Jeep's bent-in hood. The pointed toes of her shoes stuck out from under the front bumper, where her legs remained. She was cut in two and her intestines were spilling out from the lower part of her torso.

He looked up to the sky and focused on a massive white cloud as its bright intensity grew. "Sorry," he whispered. He closed his eyes and began to pray.

7

Ted lay crumpled in the back seat of the Jeep he'd hit. Pain radiated from every organ and his skin hurt the most. He could feel the hot sting of his bare muscles burning in the exposed sun. The skin on his back must have slid off when, either he flew through his windshield, or, when he smashed through the back window of the Jeep parked in the middle of the road.

He'd slowed down when he saw the hill and he couldn't have been going more than forty-five. But that was enough, obviously.

His fingers found the edge of the back seat and he was able to pull himself forward. Through the front windshield he saw her, the blonde that had nearly run him off the road earlier. She was staring right at him with dead eyes. Her mouth hung open and her intestines were slapping across the hood of her demolished vehicle.

When Ted slid across the back seat toward the door, he felt a punching sensation in his gut. Looking down, he saw a large triangle-shaped piece of the windshield embedded in his stomach. Blood leaked out all around the glass, making it look like red, melting ice. The back door fell off easily and Ted crawled out onto the street. He pulled the broken glass from his stomach, watched the blood bubble out from the wound and rested his head on the pavement.

He choked up a laugh, which strangely made his toes ache. He felt tired. Rolling over onto his stomach, he tried to push himself up to his feet. That's when he noticed the man lying in the middle of the highway, probably dead too. Looking over at his van, Ted realized that he was going to have to wait for the authorities. Then he saw himself in the shattered windshield and wondered if he would make it that long. His legs were obviously broken, so walking anywhere would be a joke. Drool slithered from between his cracked lips. Egg yolk colored stomach bile erupted from his mouth. It burned as it heaved up his throat. Then came the blood, but it appeared brown. He was bleeding internally. Falling forward against the smashed Jeep, he remembered his .44 Bulldog in the glove compartment.

It took a few minutes to pry open the passenger side door, but he got it open, grabbed the revolver. He checked the chamber to see that it was loaded. All six slots were filled. He put the barrel against the side of his head near his temple and cocked the hammer back with his thumb. With the click of the hammer, his pain seemed to diminish and something worse took over. Fear boiled in his stomach, and he found himself feeling doomed. It wasn't the paranoia he originally felt when he saw how bad the accident was. Strange as it was, it felt like when his mother had caught him being naughty as a child and the anticipation of punishment. He shrugged his shoulders, the best he could, and was about to pull the trigger when he heard the man in the road say something. His voice sounded wet.

He wanted to get this over with. The game was done, over, finished, and he wanted out. But something about the tone of this man's voice drew him in.

Winded, Ted wobbled down the highway to the man in the road.

He stopped and observed the severity of the man's injuries. This man didn't have more than a few minutes' worth of life left in him, at best.

The man started to mumble something, "I want . . . to . . . confess."

Ted let out a deep breath. It felt hot rising through his throat, and he wound up spitting blood onto the man's chest. "I ain't a priest."

"I killed . . . a boy . . ."

He killed someone? Now we're getting somewhere, Ted thought.

"I killed a boy . . . he killed my daughter . . . my Jules."

Something was oddly familiar here. *That name, "Jules."* Ted put his pain on hold and listened to the dying man. "I want to confess, before I . . . go." The dying man was fading. Ted felt a smile break out onto his face.

"You killed a boy that killed your girl?" Ted asked.

Blood exploded from the dying man's mouth, and he cried out, "I'm sorry!"

"Funny thing about this road . . . is that I met you . . . funny thing," Ted said. "That girl, Jules . . . I killed her. I took her after the boy left her for dead . . . he was a skinny boy with dark hair, right?" Ted asked, nodding his head.

The dying man's eyes went wide. "You . . . you . . . killed her?" he asked.

"She wasn't the only one." Ted laughed and his entire body shook with pain. "I think you killed the wrong guy." Ted dropped his smile and lifted the .44 Bulldog to the dying man. "Now go be with her."

There was a long silence while Ted aimed the revolver and hatred possessed the dying man's eyes. Ted could feel it.

The bullet dismantled the man's face and the contents of his head exploded across the road in a magnificent crimson splash.

Ted could barely hear a sound. The gun blast had deafened him. He put the gun to his forehead and pulled the trigger.

Ted felt his right eyeball bulge and pop. He watched the world slip as he fell to the pavement.

Chapter 29
Not Quite Adding Up

1

Tim Fuller woke up at five o'clock Friday morning with a bad stomachache. He'd experienced a few ulcers in his life, and they'd felt similar to this. He drank a cold glass of milk and tried to release his stinging bowels. His guts churned but didn't let go. After sitting on the toilet for a half an hour, nothing came out. Great. To add to his problems, he was constipated.

Normally, Tim didn't wake up until eight or a little after, but his vivid dreams last night were awful. He was walking in a field looking for his friend, Robert Grabske, but he couldn't find him. The field had small mounds scattered across it, and although there were no grave markers, he thought that he was walking through a cemetery.

He looked at the clock. It was six o'clock now. A thought popped into his mind. Out there on County Trunk A was the house that—he couldn't think of the guy's name—the one that Robert had been blubbering about at breakfast the other morning.

Ted.

Tim pushed himself up from his chair in the kitchen, stumbled over to the phone and dialed Robert's number. There was nothing but endless ringing.

Robert didn't have a cell phone and he didn't have an answering service. He was a dinosaur—much like Tim—and hadn't worried about keeping up with the times since the late 1970s.

An hour passed and Tim found himself knocking at Robert's door, hoping that he would answer with a scowl.

No luck. No Robert.

"What was his name, his full name?" Tim asked himself out loud, thinking of the man that Robert was so bent-up on. *Ted Olson.*

After an hour of driving back and forth down County Trunk A, Tim almost called it quits. Then he saw something peek out from the high grass and scattered forest.

A barn?

He saw gravel sprawled out in front of a nearly hidden path off to the left side of the road. He parked his car next to the gravel path, got out, and walked up the drive. In his old age, he had to make sure he wasn't just seeing things. He shook his head, wondering if he was back in the dream he'd had last night.

This was the field.

There was a house and a barn. The place had a strange stale odor. The faint scent of old fire permeated the humid air, like someone had been burning trash or had put out a campfire.

He walked up the porch steps to the front door and knocked. Same as at Robert's house, there was no answer, and after ten minutes or so Tim left. Walking down the gravel drive again, he looked across the tall grass and saw—like in his dream—the many small hills scattered across the field.

Maybe he should go down to the police station and report this?

He didn't want to sound blubbery, like Robert. But he couldn't find his friend, and something was amiss.

2

There were news vans, reporters, and cameramen scattered in front of the police department. It looked like a circus. Tim walked up to the main entrance. He was pushed to the side and nearly fell over after one of the cameramen backed up without looking where he was going.

"Get the hell out of the way," Tim yelled.

The cameraman looked him over and stepped aside. Tim entered through the large glass doors and found himself lost in a pond of reporters trying to get at the dispatcher, who looked about ready to quit. Her face was long, and Tim could see from across the lobby that she was sweating profusely. Then she spotted Tim, pointed at him and looked relieved. "Hello sir!"

Tim waded through the crowd toward the bullet proof glass that separated him from the dispatch desk.

She buzzed him in, and a sea of reporters tried to follow him through. Dispatch came over the microphone. "Anyone entering the restricted area will be arrested on sight . . . Chief Fuller, head on in."

Tim trudged his way through the back door and found himself swimming into another mass of people. Every officer, detective, captain, and lieutenant must have been called in today. Everyone seemed to look at him like he had an answer. Little did they—or Tim—know that he did.

3

Tim rode out to the property on County Trunk A with Captain McDonald, a barrel-chested man with a ruddy face, standing six feet four inches. His hair was thick and white, and he wore too much aftershave.

"How did you end up out here?" he asked Tim.

"Robert Grabske."

"Oh sure, I know of him. Retired in the mid-eighties . . . or so?"

"Yeah, he was babbling on about that missing girl, said she had something to do with a case we worked years ago . . . early eighties. I think he went out there to investigate . . . an old man's last attempt to do something with his life. I hadn't heard from him in more than a day, so I went looking for him. I remember Robert telling me that the guy he talked about . . . Ted Olson . . . lived out there on that road, in the sticks. The place is pretty well hidden. The only reason I saw it was because the tip of his barn stuck out above the trees. So, I checked the place out."

The captain was hanging on every word that spilled from Tim's lips. Tim felt important for the first time in a long time. It felt good to matter.

McDonald said, "We found him out on County Trunk A yesterday afternoon. Dead. Suicide. He was tangled in a wreck with the Benton family . . . the missing girl's parents."

Tim couldn't deny the coincidence. Sadness washed over him. For a lifetime career in law enforcement, he knew when things didn't feel right and now was one of those times. "I'm gonna want to file Robert Grabske missing."

Captain McDonald looked pale, and Tim could see the tiny broken purple capillaries in his face. "This isn't looking good. We also found one of our detectives at the Benton's house stabbed to death. The news media found out about it. I'm sure one of our young officers is responsible for the leak, and they're all over this."

4

It took ten minutes to drive out to Ted Olson's house. And it took an hour before they found the first body. The body belonged to Robert Grabske. Tim Fuller hadn't felt a deeper sense of loss since his wife had passed. He stayed out at the farm while a team of diggers and forensic scientists dug up the property. They put together twelve bodies by the end of the first day and thirty-two by the end of the week.

On Monday morning of the following week, Tim sat at Charlie's Diner and read the newspaper article. The caption read "*Serial Killer Sleeps Undetected in Watertown.*" Tim read on . . .

On Thursday of last week, police made a grisly discovery on County Trunk A, in Dodge County, forty miles outside of Watertown. Upon further inspection, detectives discovered that one of the deceased had died of a self-inflicted gunshot wound from a .44 caliber revolver. Further investigation led Watertown police to the property of Theodore James Olson of Watertown, a Korean war veteran who is now believed to be responsible for the deaths of over thirty-two people, including a high-profile disappearance in 1980:that of Joan Bethany Neverman, and Rodney Jacob Schmidt.

At this time, the Watertown Police Department is also uncovering a possible crime of passion in which Watertown natives, Richard and Mary Benton, were responsible for the murder deaths of Detective Peter Finley and seventeen-year-old David Miller, also of Watertown.

Police speculate that Richard and Mary Benton came to the conclusion that David Miller had killed their daughter after reading entries in her private journal. The entries may have suggested that Miller was involved. Authorities speculate that the grieving couple took the law into their own hands. A dig at Benton's Dodge County hunting property revealed the remains of David Miller.

Also, it is suspected that Mary Benton killed Detective Finley after he discovered the plot to kill

Miller. Police are still unable to determine how Ted Olson was involved with the disappearance of Jules Benton. They do speculate that Olson may have been the killer, and that the Benton's may have misjudged the situation and murdered David Miller as the result of misleading information.

5

Tim shook his head, disgusted. What had happened to the world during the short eighty-five years that he'd been alive? A seventeen-year-old girl went missing and the immediate conclusion was that the boyfriend did it. The way that Tim saw it, the Benton's had taken the law into their own hands and without due process had killed a young boy. At this point, officials didn't even know if the kid did it. Meanwhile, a serial killer enjoys a full life tucked beneath the blanket of freedom that small town living offers. No one cared about what was right anymore. People multiplied by time had evolved the truth into something that no longer existed.

Tim shook his head and asked no one, "Why do we even bother anymore?"

He slapped his newspaper together and pushed it to the far end of the table. The future didn't look very hopeful anymore and he didn't think that he cared to fight another day.

Daniel P. Coughlin was born and raised in a small town in southern Wisconsin. At the age of 19 he joined the United States Marine Corps and served four and half years as a Machine Gunner in the infantry. After being Honorably discharged, Daniel attended and graduated from California State University at Long Beach. While studying screenwriting under the mentorship of acclaimed writer Brian Alan Lane, he also interned and served as a script analyst for his favorite director, Wes Craven. *Photo by Sipper Photography*

Daniel is the author of two commercially successful films *Lake Dead*, which was selected as one of After Dark Film's *8 Films to Die For*, and *Farmhouse*, Starring A-List film and television star Steven Weber (Wings, Desperation, Single White Female). He has sold numerous short stories to such publications as *Strange Tales of Horror, Macabre Cadaver Magazine*, and *Dark Gothic Resurrected Magazine*. Daniel was hailed by *Macabre Cadaver Magazine* as, "A promising New Voice in Old School Horror."

Other HellBound Books:

Satanic Panic

"A delicious homage to those 80's horror B-movies!"

Satanic Panic, a mass hysteria created in the nineteen eighties, has returned to a small college town in the Midwest.

Ritualistic murders and the presence of the occult have bled below the surface of the town in the form of icy accidents and other coincidences.

And when three lifelong friends find themselves on the radar of a killer—and leader of a satanic cult—they must fight for what's good without being seduced by the evil that possesses their campus.

The Gentleman's Choice

"Caught in a whirlwind of adverse publicity following a viewer's death, the streaming show, The Gentleman's Choice becomes the target for a sadistic killer – and it's up to PI Vanessa Young to put a stop to it before more young women are murdered."

A sleazy internet dating show blamed for a viewer's death, a host with a dark, secret past, and a killer with a sadistic grudge…

Someone is kidnapping and murdering previous contestants from the popular streaming show *The Gentleman's Choice* – a strictly-for-adults hybrid of *The Bachelor* and *Love Island.* Private Investigator, Vanessa Young, is hired by a victim's family to infiltrate the show as a contestant to expose and capture the killer.

Vanessa and the show's charismatic star, Cole Gianni, begin to fall romantically for each other, until Vanessa's plan goes terribly awry when they're drugged and taken to a remote location to take part in their captor's own brutal, ultimately fatal, version of *The Gentleman's Choice.*

With the clock ticking toward their fateful final night, Vanessa and Cole are forced into a battle of wills to survive their tormentor and escape with their lives before it's too late…

Flanagan

"Straw Dogs meets Fifty Shades - heart pounding, gut-wrenching, sexy as all hell and with a twist you'll never see coming!"

Meet the Sewells, your typical, all-American couple; happily married for ten years, respected high school teachers, still crazy about one another and with a secret, shared dark side.

During their annual Spring Break vacation to recharge their batteries and reconnect as a couple, they are waylaid by a perverse gang of misfits in the one horse, North Texas, town of Flanagan.

Taken hostage as the focus of the gang's twisted games, the Sewells are brutalized into performing increasingly vicious physical, sexual and emotional acts upon one another, until events take an unexpected turn - triggered by an unintentional death.

As their circumstance descends into the worse nightmare imaginable, the Sewells find themselves involved in an altogether different situation...

Anthology of Splatterpunk

splat·ter·punk
noun
informal
noun: splatterpunk

Definition: "A literary genre characterized by graphically described scenes of an extremely gory nature."
HellBound Books are incredibly proud to present to you horror most raw and visceral, two-dozen suitably graphic, horrific tales of terror designed to churn the stomach and curdle the blood.
This superlative tome is an absolute must for fans of Richard Laymon, Clive Barker, Monica J. O'Rourke, Matt Shaw, Wrath James White and Jack Ketchum – all put to paper by some of the brightest new stars writing in the genre today.
Featuring stories by: Nick Clements, Carlton Herzog, NJ Gallegos, Scotty Milder, Steve Stark, Frederick Pangbourne, Cristalena Fury, Amber Willis, Kenneth Amenn, Erica Summers, Allie Guilderson, Cory Andrews, Andrew P. Weston, Shula Link, Carlton Herzog, DW Milton, Brent Bosworth, JD Fuller, Robert Allen Lupton, C.M. Noel, Julian Grant, Jay Sykes, Phil Williams, and the incomparable James H Longmore.

A HellBound Books LLC
Publication

www.hellboundbooks.com